# China's Chaplin

## Comic Stories and Farces by Xu Zhuodai

# China's Chaplin

## Comic Stories and Farces by Xu Zhuodai

Translated and with an introduction by

**CHRISTOPHER REA**

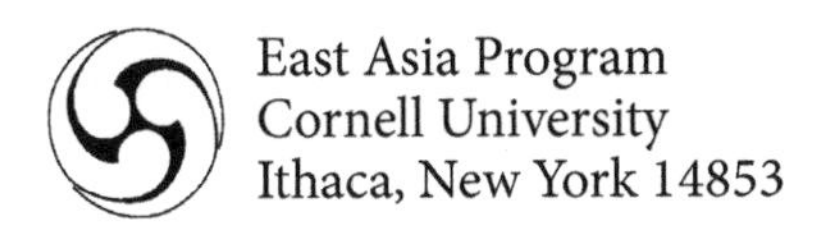

East Asia Program
Cornell University
Ithaca, New York 14853

*The Cornell East Asia Series is published by the Cornell University East Asia Program (distinct from Cornell University Press). We publish books on a variety of scholarly topics relating to East Asia as a service to the academic community and the general public. Address submission inquiries to CEAS Editorial Board, East Asia Program, Cornell University, 140 Uris Hall, Ithaca, New York 14853-7601.*

Number 194 in the Cornell East Asia Series
Copyright ©2019 Christopher Rea
All rights reserved.
ISSN: 1050-2955
ISBN: 978-1-939161-04-8 hardcover
ISBN: 978-1-939161-94-9 paperback
ISBN: 978-1-942242-94-9 e-book
Library of Congress Control Number: 2019930294

Cover: Xu Zhuodai in 1926
Image sources: *Kaixin tekan* 開心特刊 (Happy Film Company Fanzine), no. 4 (1926).
Shutterstock ID 45552427 by nicemonkey.
Cover design: Mai
Interior: Sheryl Rowe

CAUTION: Except for brief quotations in a review, no part of this book may be reproduced or utilized in any form without permission in writing from the author. Please address all inquiries to Christopher Rea in care of the East Asia Program, Cornell University, 140 Uris Hall, Ithaca, NY 14853-7601.

# Contents

## Farces

# Introduction

## "Charlie Chaplin of the East," Xu Zhuodai

Christopher Rea

Xu Zhuodai 徐卓呆 (born Xu Fulin 徐傅霖, 1880–1958) (Fig. 1) is one of those writers who could do it all.[1] Between the 1910s and the 1940s he was one of Shanghai's most prolific authors, his byline appearing in over three dozen periodicals. Need a story for your magazine's special issue on Family Life or New Year's Customs? He's your man. Do your readers fancy a certain genre? Tragedy, comedy, farce, romance, detective fiction, sci-fi, mystery, thriller—he's an old hand at each. How about an advice column? "Dr. Li Ah Mao" at your service! A translation? He's fluent in Japanese. Serialized novel? One-act play? Screenplay? Advertising tag line? Poem? Jokes, anecdotes, or gossip to fill in blank space in your journal? Xu Zhuodai could deliver all this and more.

---

1. Unless otherwise noted, sources of biographical information about Xu Zhuodai cited here can be found in chapter 5 of my book *The Age of Irreverence: A New History of Laughter in China* (Oakland, CA: University of California Press, 2015), pp. 106–131, 240–251, from which part of this introduction is adapted. The first four paragraphs are adapted from my "Introduction to Xu Zhuodai" in *Renditions* 87/88 (Spring/Autumn 2017): 189–191.

Figure 1. Xu Zhuodai in 1926. Image source: *Kaixin tekan* 開心特刊 (Happy Film Company Fanzine), no. 4 (1926).

Though a versatile writer, Xu was most famous for his knack for comedy. *An Absurd Diary* 豈有此理之日記 (1923), the poetry anthology *The Unintelligible Collection* 不知所云集 (1923), the novel *Omnipotence* 萬能術 (1926), the story collection *Drunk and Sniffing Apple Blossoms* 酒後嗅蘋果 (1929), the anthology of *Three Thousand Jokes* 笑話三千 (1935), and the story cycle *The Unofficial Story of Li Ah Mao* 李阿毛外傳 (1941–1942) are but a few of the scores of works, in various genres, that contributed to Xu's reputation for being the Laughter Artisan of the Page 文壇笑匠 and a Charlie Chaplin of the East 東方卓別林. Photos of his portly physique in costume (Fig. 2)—as a fine Western lady, perhaps, or as a thug—or in his habitual Western suit, would often appear in magazines alongside an anecdote about his latest prank on his buddies in theater, publishing or filmmaking circles.

Figure 2. Xu Zhuodai (using stage name Xu Banmei), in costume as an old man, a laborer, a Western lady, and a Chinese lady. The girl in the middle is identified as "The little New Drama actress Jade." Image source: *Yuxing* 餘興 (Amusements), Sept. 1914.

Hoaxes were Xu's specialty. Stories like "The Fiction Material Wholesaler" (1921) and "Plagiarist in Western Dress" (1923) make fun of the culture of rampant plagiarism in the Shanghai press. Bogus advertisements, fake news items, spurious notices and other media manipulations are frequent plot drivers. "Woman's Playthings" (1928) and *Li Ah Mao* stories like "Seeking Lifelong Partner" (1942) stage lonely-heart scams that target gullible urban men, for fun and profit. Xu Zhuodai's plays, too, feature scenarios such as a prostitute and her lover defrauding the young man's father; a husband and wife repeatedly locking each other out of the house late at night; and a destitute man pretending to be a ghost to extort money from his landlord and creditors.

Since seeing is *not* believing in this world, ordinary people have to become detectives. In "The Pearl Necklace," Li Ah Mao solves a jewelry heist seemingly just by reading between the lines of a newspaper report. Other stories, like "Opening Day Advertisement" 開幕廣告 (see Further Readings), reveal Xu's fondness for—but also ironic attitude toward—the procedural aesthetic of deception, detection, false leads, and revelation shared by both farce and detective fiction.

Writing was just one of the many talents of this modern Renaissance man. Xu has been hailed as a pioneer in modern physical education, spoken drama, filmmaking, and radio broadcasting. He was a man of art and of science, a cultural entrepreneur with an extroverted interest in all that the modern world had to offer. He studied physical education in Japan (picking up ballroom dancing on the side) and, with his wife Tang Jianwo 湯劍我 (d. 1932) (Fig. 3), a fellow athlete and a noted calligrapher, cofounded Shanghai's first sports academies. He started modernist theatre troupes, wrote and performed in dozens of plays, penned a newspaper column promoting drama reform, and translated numerous plays from Japanese. He cofounded two film companies and wrote China's first book on filmmaking technique, *The Science of Shadowplay* 影戲學 (1924), as well as textbooks, how-to guides, and memoirs on

Figure 3. Tang Jianwo and Xu Zhuodai in 1922. Image source: *Jiating* 家庭 (Family), no. 5 (1922).

sports physiology, Japanese martial arts, wireless radio broadcasting, music, spoken drama, stage farce, and garden design. During the war, he made ends meet by selling Li Ah Mao screenplays and running a family business manufacturing artificial soy sauce. These various enterprises brought Xu into contact with all manner of cultural celebrities. The now-legendary martial artist Huo Yuanjia 霍元甲 (1868–1910), pharmaceutical tycoon Huang Chujiu 黃楚九 (1872–1931), drama and cinema pioneer Zheng Zhengqiu 鄭正秋 (1889–1935), stage star Ouyang Yuqian 歐陽予倩 (1889–1962), future linguist and May Fourth activist Liu Fu 劉復 (1891–1934), and playwright Hong Shen 洪深 (1894–1955) are just a few of the influential cultural figures Xu worked with over the course of his career. Xu Zhuodai was a figure at the center of Republican Shanghai popular culture who knew not just everything, but everyone. The modern world, to Xu, was one of possibility and hilarity, and he invited the public to join in the fun.

> "What's today's date?"
> "I don't know. Why don't you look at that newspaper you've got there?"
> "That's no good—it's yesterday's."[2]

**MASTER OF THE BROKEN CHAMBER POT STUDIO**

Xu Zhuodai was born in Suzhou and traveled in 1902 to Japan, where he became one of the first Chinese foreign students to study physical education. While in Japan he read Western fiction in Japanese translation (later retranslating Tolstoy and Hugo from Japanese into Chinese), translated Japanese short stories and plays, and learned ballroom dancing. Returning to Shanghai a few years later, he authored introductory textbooks on gymnastics and sports physiology and, with Tang Jianwo, founded and ran two of the city's first sports academies, which graduated over 1,500 students between 1904 and 1928. A longtime theater enthusiast, Xu studied acting at a reformist drama school in the 1910s, and started a regular column in the major newspaper *The Eastern Times* 時報 in which he advocated theater reform. He was a devoted craftsman, once spending several months learning make-up techniques from a Japanese artist, and accompanying Ouyang Yuqian on a return trip to Japan in 1917 to study how actors were trained. His own stage debut in a comic role was praised by Zheng Zhengqiu, who later became his drama and film collaborator.

During his drama career, Xu wrote at least thirty short comic plays, including the six collected in this book, which is said to be

2. From Xu Zhuodai 徐卓呆, *Xiaohua sanqian* 笑話三千 (Three Thousand Jokes), vol. 1 (Shanghai: Shanghai zhongyang shudian), p. 12. Subsequent jokes are cited in text by volume and page number.

more than any other playwright of the prewar period. Though he continued writing and translating plays well into his sixties, Xu's hopes that New Drama (which emphasized spoken dialogue, rather than singing and music) could serve as a vehicle for enlightenment diminished in the late 1920s and he turned his efforts to fiction writing. He quickly gained a reputation for his funny stories, which his associates sought to ennoble by claiming, somewhat apologetically, that they were full of "truth" and "philosophical meaning." Xu said that he viewed the purpose of fiction as being to represent realistic "slices of life" and that he considered the short story to be best suited to this purpose.

Xu's writing career spanned half a century, from his earliest translations of Japanese literature while a foreign student in Japan during the 1900s, through a productive period of fiction writing from the late 1910s to the early 1940s, to memoir-writing in the early 1950s. During these decades he served a series of brief editorships at periodicals and publishing organizations such as *Shishi xinbao*, *China Books*, *New Shanghai*, and Shanghai's *Morning Post*. He published fiction in dozens of magazines and periodicals. His stories, mostly short vignettes about daily life in the city, spanned a wide variety of genres and modes, from family drama to science fiction, detective fiction, romance, and comedy. Xu's literary legacy includes over a dozen novels, scores of plays, textbooks on gymnastics and sports physiology, how-to manuals on filmmaking and radio broadcasting, a collection of parodic "new-style" poems, a pair of memoirs, numerous essays and short "space-filler" magazine pieces, and thousands of jokes (Fig. 4).

In 1924, Xu brought his comic talents from the stage and the page to the silver screen when he and fellow dramatist Wang Zhongxian 汪仲賢 (aka Wang Youyou 汪優游, 1888–1937) co-founded the Happy Film Company 開心影片公司 (Fig. 5), which specialized in slapstick shorts such as *Cupid's Fertilizer* 愛神之肥料 (1925), *Strange Doctor* 怪醫生 (1925), and *Bogus Strong Man* 假力士 (1926) (Fig. 6).

FIGURE 4. *Three Thousand Jokes* (1935).

It was a bootstrap operation. Films were shot with a second-hand camera and cast family members, as well as Xu (the "Laughter Artisan of the Page") and Wang (the "Laughter Artisan of the Stage") themselves, in over two dozen films. By the mid-1920s a market for slapstick film had been well established in China, with the films of Harold Lloyd and Charlie Chaplin spawning local imitators, such as Zhang Shichuan's 張石川 (1890–1954) *The King of Comedy's Journey to Shanghai* 滑稽大王游滬記 (1921), in which a British resident of Shanghai played the Little Tramp. Unfortunately, Xu and Wang's foray into filmmaking coincided with a

FIGURE 5. The logo for Happy Film Company (ca. 1925–1926): Piggy (Zhu Bajie) swallowing a key to open the heart, *kaixin*, that is, become Happy. Image source: *Kaixin tekan*, no. 4 (1926).

general shift in audience tastes away from the gag-and-novelty-driven "cinema of attractions" and toward narrative feature film. By Xu's account, the company folded due to poor reviews and the low market price of funny shorts relative to longer feature films. A second joint effort, the Candle Film Company, met a similar demise. Over the course of his career in cinema, however, Xu wrote some of China's earliest books on filmmaking and cinematography. He remained in demand as a screenwriter as late as 1940, when he was contracted to write a series of film screenplays based on one of his fictional characters, Li Ah Mao.

Xu was a living embodiment of the Chinese truism that "the writing mirrors the writer" (*ren ru qi wen* 人如其文). A born performer, his exuberance extended beyond the stage and screen to his own public persona. His contemporary Yan Fusun 嚴芙孫 (b. 1901) remarked in 1923 that "at age 43, he actually looked only 33, wrote stories which seemed written by a 23-year-old, joked with the lightheartedness of someone 13, and, if he really tried, could make himself up and effectively imitate the speech and laughter of a 3-year-old."

Like the American impresario P.T. Barnum, Xu was both a

FIGURE 6. A production still from the film *Bogus Strong Man* (1924), appearing in a fanzine of the Happy Film Company. Xu Zhuodai is at left.

connoisseur of humbug and an inventive and tireless self-promoter. He adopted different comic alter egos at different stages of his career, many based on linguistic puns or contradictory double meanings. Born Xu Fulin 徐傅霖, in the theater and film worlds he went by Xu Banmei 徐半梅 ("half plum"), a visual pun on "plum" (*mei* 梅), which was originally written as two *dai* 呆 characters (*mei* 槑). His pen name, Zhuodai, which pairs *zhuo*

> "How many sons do you have, Mr. Zhang?"
>
> "Ai! It's such a pity. My grandfather-in-law kept trying to arrange a marriage for my father-in-law but my father-in-law never agreed to a match, so he never married my mother-in-law who consequently never gave birth to my wife. That's why I don't have a single son!" (1, 56)

卓 (literally "outstanding," but also a homophone for "clumsy") and *dai* 呆 ("stupid"), is self-deprecating but also hints that he is "above the common herd" (*zhuo er bu qun* 卓而不群). He also converted his original name, Xu Fulin, into Zhuo Fuling 卓弗靈, "Dim-witted Chaplin," which punned on Charlie Chaplin's Chinese name, Zhuo Bielin 卓別林 (also given 卓別霖 / 卓別靈), and alluded to his own reputation as a Chaplin of the East. His many other self-administered titles included Master of the Broken Chamberpot Studio 破夜壺室主 and, in his comic martial arts novel, *Red Pants, the Woman Warrior* 女俠紅褲子 (1930), Dr. Split-Crotch Pants 開襠褲博士, referring to the garment Chinese children wore for easy evacuation. In the 1940s after he and his second wife, Hua Duancen 華端岑, set up a factory that produced artificial soy sauce he adopted a pen name drawn from an opera about a humble artisan who wins the love of a famous courtesan: Soy Sauce Seller 賣油郎.

Xu stayed in the public eye in no small part thanks to his nose for novelty. When the infamous "Dr. Sex," Zhang Jingsheng 張競生 (1888–1970), published his sensational collection of *Sex Histories* (*Xingshi* 性史) in 1926, Xu Zhuodai and Ping Jinya 平襟亞 (1892–1978) came out soon afterward with a send-up entitled *The Art of Sex* (*Xingyi* 性藝). In this parody, which may no longer be extant, a certain inexperienced "Dr. Zhang" places an ad in the newspaper seeking sexual partners, ostensibly to advance the field of sexology. He ends up beset by a series of adventurous women—mistresses, widows, nuns, actresses, and the like—each with her own special sexual skill, who treat him as a gigolo. The last woman brings a dog that bites off Dr. Zhang's "Little Doctor," and he dies of his injuries, a martyr to scientific inquiry.[3]

As this overview of his career suggests, Xu Zhuodai was a

---

3. The work is mentioned in a 1961 essay by Xu Bai 徐白 entitled "Doufu zuojia Xu Zhuodai" 豆腐作家徐卓呆 (Tofu Writer Xu Zhuodai), which is reprinted in his book *Qingzun zaitan* 傾尊再談 (Taipei: Zhuanji wenxue chubanshe, 1969), pp. 32–41. Xu Bai claims that *The Art of Sex* appeared

FIGURE 7. A caricature of Xu Zhuodai, featured as #2 in a series of the "108 Leaders of Shanghai Literature" in the Shanghai tabloid *Jeep* 吉普 no. 15 (1946). The caption calls him "Dr. Do-It-All, A Man of Innumerable Clever Tricks."

"Chinese Chaplin" in that he was famous for being funny. Comedy, as Xu's brand, extended beyond the texts he created to his public reputation as comic icon. Whereas Chaplin was a global celebrity, Xu's sphere of influence—despite having a national readership—appears to have been primarily regional. He was Shanghai's funny man-about-town (Fig. 7). As a comedian of the silver screen, Xu's career was relatively short and remains obscure. None of his films survive, and his acting skills can be inferred only from testimonials of friends and a few extant production shots. The latter reveal that his face, like Chaplin's, was expressive, but the two men's screen presence was quite different. Xu's bald head and rotund

---

pseudonymously in 1925, but Zhang Jingsheng's *Sex Histories* only appeared in 1926, and I have not been able to find the original. My thanks to Leon Rocha for sharing Xu Bai's work with me.

physique make for a roly-poly look that differs starkly from Chaplin's skinny and diminutive Little Tramp. In any event, cinema played a relatively small part in Xu's career, and his fame as a screen comedian was less than that of actors such as Liu Jiqun 劉繼群 (1908–1940), Han Langen 韓蘭根 (1909–1982), Yin Xiucen 殷秀岑 (1911–1979), and Zheng Zhengqiu, who were routinely likened to Western icons such as Chaplin, Harold Lloyd, and Laurel and Hardy. Xu Zhuodai nevertheless shares with Chaplin not only a career-long dedication to comedy but the savvy of a self-promoting businessman. Xu is notable as a representative of an increasingly prevalent mode of urban cultural practice of cultural entrepreneurship, a pluralistic approach to culture as business spanning multiple forms of cultural production. Many of his comic stories involve the creative use, abuse, and manipulation of modern mass media to give the public what it *thinks* it wants.

## MAKING SHANGHAI A FUNNY PLACE

Xu Zhuodai was one of a new crop of writers promoting a vision of the city as a "funny" (*huaji* 滑稽) place, a farcical arena filled with mountebanks and other slippery characters. Xu was not alone in this enterprise. According to the literary historian Fan Boqun 范伯群, "virtually every single author of modern popular literature wrote comic works, the only question being how many." Fellow comic writers based in Shanghai included writers Cheng Zhanlu 程瞻廬 (1879/82–1943), Geng Xiaodi 耿小的 (1907–1994), Gong Shaoqin 貢少芹 (1879–1939), Wu Shuangre 吳雙熱 (1884–1934), and Wang Zhongxian.

Shanghai, the city in which Xu Zhuodai's varied career flourished, was also one of his major sources of comic inspiration. This most modern of Chinese cities could be discombobulating, engendering an acute sense of incongruity among visitors and residents alike. The rapidly growing metropolis boasted a modern infrastructure, a burgeoning popular press, a welter of mass entertainment options, and a cosmopolitan sensibility influenced by the presence of the settlements—large tracts of the city that operated under foreign law. Migrants from around the country poured into Shanghai in the early twentieth-century, boosting demand for entertainment periodicals and added a mix of dialects to Shanghai's linguistic stew of Mandarin, Shanghainese, Suzhou lilt, Ningbo twang, French, English, German, Russian, and "foreign settlement pidgin." Families packed in together in apartment buildings and row houses, new but cramped modern living spaces that made getting to know the neighbors—sometimes through squabbling, spying, or eavesdropping—a part of daily life. The streets also offered their own attractions, a kaleidoscopic spectacle from rag-picking beggars to high-heeled flappers to turbaned Sikh policemen to bigwigs in flashy cars.

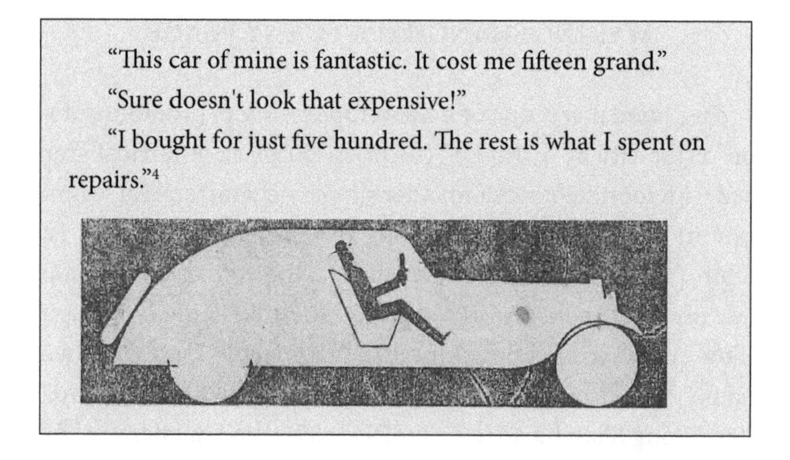

"This car of mine is fantastic. It cost me fifteen grand."
"Sure doesn't look that expensive!"
"I bought for just five hundred. The rest is what I spent on repairs."[4]


Newspaper reporters, authors and editors, office workers, modern girls, petty entrepreneurs, roadside fortunetellers, prosti-

4. Xu Zhuodai 徐卓呆 (text), Zhou Hanming 周汗明 (illustrations), *Xiaohua xiao hua* 笑話笑画 (Jokes with Cartoons). Shanghai: Zhongyang shudian, 1938, p. 24. Subsequent cartoons in the introduction are from this book.

tutes, unemployed men, and wealthy tycoons are a few of the urban walks of life represented in Xu Zhuodai's stories and plays.

Shanghai writers of the late nineteenth and early twentieth century often referred to their city as a "playground" 游戲場 of courtesans, literary games, and various sorts of whimsical role playing. Beginning in the 1910s, entrepreneurs fueled growing demand for affordable diversions by opening multistory amusement halls featuring peep shows, freak shows, comic plays, acrobatic performances, storytellers, balladeers, fortunetellers, teahouses, snack shops, rooftop gardens, and a variety of other attractions. (In "Marrying Indirectly," Lechy Lao falls in love with a girl he spotted at an amusement hall.) Comic films such as *Piggy Visits Shanghai* 豬八戒游滬記 (1927) and *Modern Crazy Ji* 現代濟公 turned Shanghai into a realm of picaresque adventure, drawing on familiar comic figures from traditional stories to convey the bizarre mix of old and new, Chinese and foreign that one encountered on a daily basis in the metropolis. The delusions and superstitions of naïve migrants were mocked in satires such as Zhang Tianyi's 張天翼 (1906–1985) novel *The Pidgin Warrior* 洋涇浜奇俠 (1936). Wang Zhongxian and cartoonist Xu Xiaoxia 許曉霞 teamed up to publish a glossary of *Shanghai Slang Illustrated and Explained* 上海俗語圖說 (1935), which taught recent arrivals how to understand the lingo and avoid being taken for *Amulin* 阿木林 (a moron). Xu's stories are dotted with such slang.

> Tenant: I really can't stand that bloke in the flat above. Last night he just wouldn't stop stomping around.
>
> Landlord: Sorry about that, I'll have a word with him. Oh, by the way, how do you spend your time down here?
>
> Tenant: I practice the trombone.[5]

5. My thanks to Paul Bevan for bringing this joke of Xu Zhuodai's to my attention.

FIGURE 9. *Jokes with Cartoons* (1938), written by Xu Zhuodai and illustrated by Zhou Hanming.

Cartoons became a staple of urban print culture, appearing both in newspapers and in dedicated cartoon magazines such as *Shanghai Sketch* 上海漫畫, *Oriental Puck* 獨立漫畫, *Comics Life* 漫畫生活, *Modern Sketch* 現代漫畫, and *Funny Cartoons* 滑稽漫畫. In the 1930s Ye Qianyu's 葉淺予 (1907–1995) comic strip *Mr. Wang* 王先生 became a hit for capturing the Shanghainese stereotypes of the "behind-the-times traditionalist" and the "fake foreign devil" in its heroes, Mr. Wang and Little Chen. The Li Ah Mao stories were illustrated, and he too became a recognizable face in films based on the character. Shanghai, as the center of Republican China's publishing and cinema industries, had an outsized influence on modern Chinese culture. It especially influenced the history of comedy, most notably in 1932, when Lin Yutang 林語堂 (1895–1976) and a group of other famous writers living in Shanghai launched a humor magazine, *The Analects Fortnightly* 論語半月刊, which became a nationwide sensation and turned *youmo* 幽默 (humor) into the household word it remains today.

Xu Zhuodai's writings give us a taste of what one comedian found so funny about Shanghai, about China, and about modern life in general. They reveal a farcical sensibility that appealed to a broad population of urban readers and audiences. The plays and stories in this collection were first published the 1920s, with the exception of *The Unofficial Story of Li Ah Mao*, which was serialized during the Japan's occupation of Shanghai during World War II. In them we find a topsy-turvy world in which tricksters reign supreme, and in which readers and people on the street alike need to remain ever vigilant.

## THE STORIES

Written in an accessible vernacular and sprinkled with Shanghainese expressions and joke names (some of which I've glossed at the back of this book), Xu Zhuodai's stories present a comic take on the workings of the modern city. His main characters are typically scrappy underdogs—likeable tricksters or well intentioned confidence (wo)men working to help themselves and their friends. Through their escapades, readers learn imaginative ways to exploit or circumvent the city's cultural institutions for one's own ends. In "Woman's Playthings," for example, a female writer solicits a husband from among her newspaper readers, only to trick away respondents' money and make them publicly confront their collective foolishness. Litman Deng, the proprietor in "The Fiction Material Wholesaler," is revealed to be perpetrating an unintentional hoax on his customers, all would-be writers eager to join Shanghai's overheated fiction market. Through scams, swindles, and practical jokes, Xu Zhuodai leads his readers along a comic narrative arc from deception to revelation.

Many of these trickster figures hail from the entertainment and mass media circles Xu Zhuodai knew so well. The title character in "The Marketing Director" is employed by a publishing house, while "Woman's Playthings" dangles before us the question of the true identity of Miss Qiu Suwen, a mysterious poet, painter, and calligrapher. We also encounter the titular literary entrepreneur of "The Fiction Material Wholesaler," and, in "Plagiarist in Western Dress," an alter ego of Xu Zhuodai himself. Through these stories, Xu lets us see Shanghai's profusion (and confusion) of multiple forms of cultural production, including literature, drama, comics, print advertising, and film as integral to everyday life—albeit in unexpected ways. As a practitioner in these fields, Xu used fiction to register his amusement at how the allure and anonymity of various media could be exploited for individual gain. These stories caution urbanites in search of stimulation: keep your guard up or you might end up making a spectacle of yourself!

In targeting gullible readers Xu aimed to deflate the public's reverence for the written word by revealing the inner workings of

the cultural institutions, such as the newspaper, which his readership looked to for education and entertainment. Deceptive practices such as plagiarism had created an identity crisis in the city's cultural circles. How to determine who's who or who's written what? At times, Xu draws on the conventions of detective fiction to promote a deductive approach to solving the city's mysteries, as in the Li Ah Mao stories "Turned Around" and "The Pearl Necklace." Yet even when being critical or sarcastic, Xu differs from many satirists of the period in that he indulges rather than condemns such readerly conceits, pointing out the folly of confusing fiction for reality while at the same time enabling his readers to reimagine the city in terms that are not strictly realistic.

Indeed, far from simply admonishing readers, Xu's stories also promote a particular model of cultural hero-cum-urban legend who is closely tied to Xu's own public persona: the trickster. The most extended articulation of this trope appears in *The Unofficial Story of Li Ah Mao*, a series of twelve stories that were serialized monthly between July 1941 and June 1942. This one-year period spanned the December 1941 bombing of Pearl Harbor, after which the Japanese extended their occupation of Shanghai from Chinese-administered districts into the formerly "neutral" foreign settlements. Once an "orphan island," Shanghai now fell completely under the administration of the Japanese military government.

The stories are linked by a swindler named Li Ah Mao who uses inventive methods of obtaining food and money for his poor friends, evincing an overarching thematic concern with survival in a precarious urban environment. War and the Japanese occupation are alluded to only indirectly: "Please Exit Through the Back Door" mentions soaring inflation and "Japanese School" notes the presence of Japanese people in the city. If the title *The Unofficial Story of Li Ah Mao* brings to mind Lu Xun's famous novella *The True Story of Ah Q* 阿Q正傳 (1921), Ah Mao, too, was a cultural icon, albeit with important differences from Ah Q. Whereas the petty bully Ah Q's opportunism was yet another symptom of cultural backwardness, Ah Mao's marked him as a man of his times. In Xu's occupied Shanghai, opportunism was not self-destructive behavior, but a shrewd mode of agency by which one could survive and thrive in an age of mass media and material deprivation.

By the time the first Li Ah Mao stories were published, Ah Mao was already more than a fictional character—he was a franchise. Like Ye Qianyu's cartoon character "Mr. Wang," who became the central character in at least a dozen live-action (as opposed to animated) films, Li Ah Mao made the leap from page to screen. Xu had invented Ah Mao in the 1930s as an alter ego for a newspaper column in which he fielded any question readers put to him. The column proved so popular that he was approached by the Guohua Film Company, which proposed making a series of movies based on the character. At least three films were produced: *Li Ah Mao and Miss Tang* 李阿毛與唐小姐 (1939), *Li Ah Mao and the Zombie* 李阿毛與殭屍 (1940), and *Li Ah Mao and Dongfang Shuo* 李阿毛與東方朔 (1940), for each of which Xu himself penned the screenplay. These films fared much better at the box office than Xu's own Happy Film Co. productions. *Li Ah Mao and Dongfang Shuo*, for instance, ranked as the sixth-highest-grossing film in the first half of 1940, and prompted one reviewer to remark that "every little kid knows the three words 'Li Ah Mao.'" With an audience in place, Li Ah Mao became one of Xu's most popular literary creations.

"Please Exit Through the Back Door" (1942) illustrates the Ah Mao ethos. In the story, Ah Mao is approached by two recently unemployed friends who ask him to save them from imminent poverty. Ah Yang owns a garden supply store, but in a time when people can barely afford rice, business has plummeted and he has been forced to close shop. Ah Ping's barbershop, which shares a back door with Ah Yang's shop, has been suffering similar difficulties. Ah Mao sets a get-rich-quick scheme in motion by taking out two advertisements in the newspaper: one saying that Ah Yang's shop is selling a "fast-acting miracle hair-growth tonic" and another saying that Ah Ping's barbershop is selling the secret to a "new, super-economical head-shaving method." After the advertisements appear, customers throng the front door of each shop, but the "miracle cures" they've come to seek turn out to be miraculous only in their clever marketing.

The joke turns on two "optical illusions," one textual and one physical. The former is akin to the deceptive advertisements for "miracle cures" that frequently appeared in early Republican periodicals. Huang Chujiu's best-selling "Ailuo Brain Tonic," Dr. William's Pink Pills for Pale People, and Chen Diexian's 陳碟仙 Human Elixir (*rendan* 人丹, an imitation of a Japanese product called Humane Elixir, *rendan* 仁丹) are among the dubious remedies that were widely advertised in newspapers across China in Xu Zhuodai's age. The physical optical illusion (the mechanics of which I will not reveal here) involves the arrangement of the city street as a performative space by turning storefronts into stages for a public audience of passersby and teahouse patrons. The two optical illusions, in turn, are validated through the gossip mill, which helps the public internalize the original print-based hoax.

> Tiger Balm King Aw Boon Haw never used to advertise, claiming, "I don't believe anyone pays attention to ads; if they did, I'd pay to advertise daily." A newspaper got wind of this and printed the headline "What will Aw Boon Haw do?" This prompted Aw to inquire with the publisher, who told him: "See tomorrow's paper." The next day's headline read: "Aw Boon Haw will begin advertising." And from then on, Aw advertised daily. (1, 38)

Xu's fictional comic arena was thus closely tied to his own various occupations as a writer, playwright, editor, actor, advertiser, and educator. His hoaxes represent the apex of a comedic reimagining of cultural agency in modern Shanghai, deriving their comic appeal, in part, from the author's exploitation of the print medium—the cultural context he shares with his readers. As an inventor of fictional tricksters and as a trickster himself, Xu approximates what literary scholar Edith Kern calls the "quintessence of the absolute comic" who "transports us into worlds where imagination and make-believe triumph." Modern urban life was a joke to Xu Zhuodai, but a joke of his own making.

## THE FARCES

*China's Chaplin* also presents six original translations of stage farces from the 1920s. These plays, originally published in 1923 and 1924 in the magazine *The Story World*, offer a window into the theatrical side of Xu Zhuodai's comic imagination. The 1920s was a period of dramatic growth and experimentation for modern Chinese theater, as foreign-educated reformers (Xu included) appropriated Japanese and Western dramatic forms to reinvigorate the Chinese stage. Short, one-act skits such as the ones translated here would provide actors a basis for comic improvisation and might also be adapted to become scenes in locally produced films. Of these plays, four were originally dubbed farces (*xiaoju* 笑劇) and two, *Upstairs, Downstairs: Two Couples* and *The Horse's Tail*, comedies (*xiju* 喜劇). The term comedy here applies broadly, since the mode of *Upstairs, Downstairs* alternates parody with travesty and the form of *The Horse's Tail* closely resembles the Beijing-style repartee-based stand-up comedy known as "face-and-voice," or *xiangsheng* 相聲.

In contrast with his stories, many of which comment on contemporary print media culture, Xu's plays focus on traditional comic themes, such as drunkenness, poverty, domestic quarrels, intergenerational conflict over marriage, and the beleaguered man trying to cheat hardship and death. Read in tandem with the stories, they reveal cross-genre connections in the use of the hoax mechanism and in such themes as the hen-pecked husband's revenge on domineering wife in *After the Banquet*, a premise Xu revisited two decades later in the Li Ah Mao story "The Lockout."

The idiom of these plays can be illustrated through a few brief examples. In *The Devil Messenger* (1923) the destitute Ah Ba has welcomed the God of Fortune every New Year only to find himself poorer at year's end. Changing tactics, this year he prays to the God of Misfortune. A friend who overhears his lament dresses up as a devil and tells Ah Ba that he will die at midnight. Deciding to make the most of his remaining hours, Ah Ba borrows money from his landlord and orders himself a banquet, a set of funeral clothes, and a coffin. Drunk, he dons the funeral garb and falls asleep in the coffin, snoring loudly. Surprised to find himself still alive the next morning, Ah Ba frightens his creditors into giving him more "funeral gifts." As he continues carousing, the "devil" returns and demands a bribe to not take him to the underworld. Ah Ba shares his feast with the devil, who gets drunk and betrays his true identity. Ah Ba is ready to beat him, but the friend points out that it is he who is to thank for Ah Ba's sudden wealth. So reconciled, the two keep drinking until the creditors return, discover the hoax, and trick the panicked pair to hide together in the coffin, which they nail shut and trundle off. Movement, noise, and action drive the play's comic energy. The pace is quick, with many the exits and entrances typical of slapstick farce. Ah Ba himself is repeatedly climbing in and out of the coffin—putting

> FATHER: "Who do you want marry when you grow up?"
> SON: "I want to marry granny. She loves me the most."
> FATHER: "Ridiculous! Your granny is my mother! How could you marry her?"
> SON: "And just why can't I marry your mother? You married mine!"(1, 55)

in a mattress and food, peeking out to count the dishes arriving for him, smoking and drinking, and then hiding again. The exaggerated physicality conveys the desperate fatalism of inescapable poverty.

> When English humorist George Bernard Shaw visited Shanghai [in February 1933], a beautiful woman drove over to meet him. She joked to him: "If you and I were to get married, our children would be—according to the theory of eugenics—as intelligent as you and as beautiful as me." Shaw replied: "But what a disaster it would be if they turned out as beautiful as me and as intelligent as you!" (1, 105)

*Upstairs, Downstairs: Two Couples* (1923) presents a buffoonish travesty of modern, upper-class free courtship.

A young man and woman, Mr. Shameless and Miss Parrot, meet on a park bench, hold hands, profess their mutual affection, and, having each assured the other that their father will not object to the match, agree to marry and go off to lunch. Their exchange is witnessed by their servants, a chauffeur and a maid, who separately observe them from behind a tree. When the first couple leaves the park, the servants come out from their hiding places one at a time and declare their own resolve to find a mate. Both return bizarrely dressed, and reenact the earlier courtship scene, with the man reading gibberish from a foreign book to display his cosmopolitan sophistication to his lady love. In the "upstairs" courtship, Shameless regales Parrot with modern notions about free love, expounding on youthful desire as a violent passion that society should not repress. In the "downstairs" courtship, Lucky, the chauffeur, speaks of courtship in terms of defecation ("our love is deeper than a cesspool"), sex ("my local temple god has always approved of me whoring around"), and eating ("your tummy

rumbly?")—a carnivalesque trinity that degrades love to pure physiology. The following scene, set in a Western-style restaurant, is a similar mix of exaggerated affectation. In the finale, Shameless and Parrot are standing before the altar when their servants burst in and misrecognize master and mistress for their own lover. In the end, the servants spot each other and are welcomed by the ensemble as "another married couple."

The play mocks the stylized courtship pretensions of the urban upper class, whose manners are exaggerated and parodied to the point of absurdity. The misrecognitions of the bride and groom in the final scene also raises the question of just how different the masters are from their servants. Yet the focus of the play is clearly on the "downstairs" couple, who are granted more stage time and who enact an imagined social ascent by assuming the trappings of their master and mistress. In the end, their play-act is treated benignly and the assembled wedding attendees approve their love-match. Like in *The Devil Messenger*, in *Upstairs, Downstairs* members of the lower class enjoy a temporary respite from their work obligations and inferior social status. In the meantime, Happy's "fooling around for a while with a co-ed" offers us the vicarious pleasure of seeing the upper crust through vulgar eyes.

Plays like *A Father's Duty* (1924) indicate the continued appeal of traditional comic themes in an age flirting with the modern, such as the conflict between personal desire and Confucian duty. A young man, Dandy Chen, and his father, Kway See Chen encounter each other at the entrance to a brothel. Each dispatches the other with the excuse that he just happened to be passing by, only to return separately and sneak into the brothel one after another. Dahlia the prostitute receives son and father in turn. Dandy informs Dahlia of his plan to trick his greedy father into allowing them to marry by talking up his fiancée's large dowry. When his father, Kway See, arrives, Dandy hides in the wardrobe and overhears his father tell Dahlia of his plan to marry her once his son is married off. She feigns delight and convinces Kway See to give her three thousand dollars to prepare for their wedding and settle her debts. In the final scene, Dandy's bride is revealed to be none other than Dahlia herself, and since Kway See won't admit his relationship with Dahlia in front of the wedding party, the couple succeeds in relieving the old man of both his money and his concubine. Like another of Xu's plays, *Marrying Indirectly* (1924), *A Father's Duty* playfully inverts the traditional family ethics of the Confucian father-son relationship, sharing with *The Devil Messenger* a sense of comic justice in which the

> FATHER: Son, you're a man now. It's time you took a wife.
>
> SON: I want to, daddy, but the world is such a vast place that I don't know whose wife to take. (1, 107)

original trickster (in this case, the father marrying off his son for his own selfish purposes) gets outmaneuvered at the end.

* * *

As a whole, *China's Chaplin* introduces a different voice from the somber and plaintive strains found in many literary anthologies of modern China. Comedy in China, while highly prized for its commercial value, has historically been considered a literary mode unworthy of or unamenable to criticism. Satire has been the chief exception to this rule among literary critics, who have extolled its supposed efficacy in correcting wayward behavior. Xu Zhuodai's works represent a mode of imagination that drew upon and spoke to a wide range of the modern urban experience, but without the pretense of correcting anyone. While making hay of daydreaming fools, petty crooks, old lechers, and grasping landlords, Xu's comedy is emphatically cosmic in its concern with inclusiveness, symmetry, and resolution through comic justice. Rather than simply condemn social deviance, Xu's works imagine the modern city as a domain in which there is more than enough fun and folly to go around.

I would like to thank Mai Shaikhanuar-Cota, the managing editor of the Cornell East Asia Series, for accepting this book for publication, Amy Odum for copyediting, and Sheryl Rowe for the stylish layout. Patricia Rea proofread the entire book. Thanks, Mom! I would also like to thank Ted Huters, Liu Yuqing, and two anonymous reviewers for their comments on the manuscript. I am grateful to the Social Sciences and Humanities Research Council of Canada, which funded some of the research that went into this book. My thanks, as always, to Julie, Peregrin, and Permenia for their love and support.

Happy reading!

# Author's Preface

Whereas.............................moreover........................ .........................not..........................yet..................... ...furthermore...............of............naturally.............. ............whither..........also......................certainly......... ........those...............too.........................so.................... .............why................wherefore.............saying........... ...to................although..........................their................. ........................................indeed.

Composed by Zhuodai in the Broken Chamberpot Studio on the day the butterflies' marriage was announced, October 1935.

# STORIES

# Woman's Playthings

I

Miss Qiu Suwen's poems and essays had already been appearing in various newspapers and magazines for three months when two of her works came on display at an art exhibition. Visitors no sooner saw her painting of flowers on a hanging scroll and her decorative couplet in the stone-drum inscription style than it became common knowledge that Miss Qiu was not only a talented writer but a calligrapher and a painter as well. Yet no one had ever seen Miss Qiu in the flesh, and the public had no idea whether she was beautiful or ugly. Fans of her works had searched high and low to get the inside scoop on her, but their various efforts to locate either her or anyone who knew her had all come up short. This led many people to speculate that Miss Qiu wasn't a local but rather a sojourner—and she must be a new arrival, since no one's ever heard of her!

As society was groping about in the dark for clues about the real Miss Qiu Suwen, a notice suddenly appeared in the newspaper saying that she was seeking a husband. Readers were uniformly shocked at this announcement, but from its contents they were still unable to glean any details about her.

The advertisement read:

**Miss Qiu Suwen Seeks a Husband**

*Miss Qiu's learning and talent need no introduction. She now hopes to choose a compatible spouse and invites interested parties to post a letter to P.O. Box X.*

The advertisement specified no particular conditions, so every young lad who read it bent over his desk and wrote a letter to Miss Qiu Suwen. As a result, just three days after the notice appeared, her post office box was stuffed with a grand total of 1,234 letters.

## II

Over the next few days, Miss Qiu Suwen mailed a reply to each of those 1,234 letters per the return address on the envelope. Imagine the delight of each recipient at receiving this fragrant missive! To his greater delight, on the upper left-hand corner of each letter was pasted a small photo of a beautiful young woman beneath the caption: "A portrait of Suwen." The penmanship of the letter was delicate and exquisite—clearly Miss Qiu's own hand. Her letter read:

*My Dear Mr. So-and-so: I read your letter aloud to myself with delight. Let us meet in the park on the 13th of this month at 3 pm. Please wear a small red flower on your lapel. I will be the woman in green.*

*See you there, Qiu Suwen*

Each recipient of this letter was beside himself with joy. Had he known that 1,233 other people had received the exact same letter, his joy would have vanished instantly.

At 3:00 p.m. on the 13th, the park was suddenly packed with over a thousand people—young and old, handsome and hideous, ordinary and extraordinary. Upon closer inspection, each could be seen to be sporting a small red flower. The situation was rather awkward, with everyone staring at each other, so each man renewed his search for the woman in green. By 5:00 p.m., however, no woman in green had materialized, so there was nothing for the men to do but to beat a hasty retreat.

The next day, each man received the following letter from Qiu Suwen:

*My Dear Mr. So-and-so: Yesterday I sent one of my girlfriends in advance to visit the park, where she saw an enormous crowd of people, each wearing a small red flower. You must have orchestrated a practical joke by having a big group of your friends show up just to embarrass me. Alas! The lovesick flower sheds petals, but the heartless stream flows ever on. Henceforth, please cease all communications!*

*Qiu Suwen*

Receiving such a letter, each man flew into a panic—little knowing that his letter was but one of 1,234! Each wrote a response in haste. Some claimed that it was a misunderstanding on her part, while others argued forcefully that he had nothing to do with this affair. Some cursed the God of Gambling for their rotten luck, while others asked her to set another date for them to meet. Having already obtained Qiu Suwen, how could any man bear to let her go?

## III

A few days later, each suitor received another letter from Miss Qiu Suwen, which read:

*On the 29th of this month at 3 pm, please meet me at Stars of the Silver Screen Cinema. I will again wear green. Whatever you do, don't miss our date!*

*Qiu Suwen*

Receiving this letter, each man's disappointment turned to delight, and on the afternoon of the 29th, Stars of the Silver Screen Cinema was packed to a full house. Yet the moviegoers were too busy looking about in the darkness to pay any attention to the action onscreen. As soon as the lights went up at intermission, the search became even more desperate, but of the woman in green there was not a trace. Even though every man waited until the cinema closed, Miss Qiu Suwen never appeared. Truly bizarre!

*Will she be a no-show again, just like at the park?* each date thought to himself. *It sure is crowded here, but the other people appear to be just regular moviegoers. She couldn't accuse me of a perpetrating another hoax, could she?*

Pity these clueless fellows! Each returned home utterly mystified and harboring his own suspicions. The next day, each opened the newspaper to see the following item:

*Social butterfly Miss Qiu Suwen was en route to meet a friend at Stars of the Silver Screen Cinema yesterday when her car was struck by another vehicle and she was thrown to the pavement. Fortunately, she was aided by a passerby who took her to the hospital for treatment. The doctors report that she suffered no serious injuries, apart from slight skin abrasions on her arms, and that she should be fully recovered after three or four days of quiet rest.*

Reading this, each man suddenly saw the light: *Ha ha! So that's it! No wonder she didn't show. What a shame that she's suffered so much on my account.*

All of the men felt sorry for Qiu Suwen, but, unfortunately for them, they couldn't pay her a visit because they didn't know which hospital to go to.

The big joke on those infatuated men was that Miss Qiu Suwen had spent sixty dollars to rent out Stars of the Silver Screen Cinema on the 29th and sold them all tickets. Just imagine: had they known, they'd have gone *crazy* with anger! Had they also known that Miss Qiu grossed over four hundred and eighty dollars, netting over four hundred dollars after expenses, they'd have been *sick* with anger! And had they known that Miss Qiu used those four hundred dollars to treat half a dozen of her girlfriends to an outing to Hangzhou's West Lake, they'd have *died* of anger!

## IV

When Miss Qiu Suwen returned from Hangzhou, her post office box was again jammed with letters. Opening them one by one, she learned that the men all had their doubts as to who she really was, and after two no-shows on her part she was reproached by not a few. By way of conclusion, each asked Miss Qiu to send him her address post haste, advising that if she failed to do so it would be a sign that she was nothing but an insincere playgirl.

At this point, Miss Qiu Suwen had no option but to provide an address, so she wrote replies to each. And just *what* did she write in these letters, you ask? Would she willingly tell them her address and be inundated with a thousand-plus visitors? No! Her reply was remarkable!

"This is my mailing address" she told B, giving him A's address. To C she gave B's address, claiming, "This is my humble abode." And so on: C's address went to D, and D's address went to E—all told she mailed 1,234 different addresses in lieu of her own to 1,234 different people.

Naturally, as soon as these men who hungered after Miss Qiu Suwen received her address, each went to call on her in person. As a result, F went to G's house looking for Miss Suwen, while H sought *Mi-su* [Miss] Qiu at I's place. For three or four solid days they ran back and forth like this, causing a delightful brouhaha and leaving everyone completely baffled. Little did they know that over one thousand men had been sent on several laps of a wild goose chase simply by a flash of the pen of delicate, little Miss Qiu Suwen!

## V

As for Miss Qiu Suwen's true identity, nobody at the time had any clue whatsoever.

In fact, Miss Qiu Suwen was a fifty-six-year-old widow. Her grandson had already graduated from university, and the photograph in the letter was that of her granddaughter who had passed away the previous year.

Had those thousand-plus men known the truth, they'd never have fallen for her tricks.

# The Fiction Material Wholesaler

## I

FICTION MATERIAL WHOLESALER
"Advocating Art & Literature
Promoting Domestic Goods"

Litman Deng, Proprietor

Ever since hanging out its shingle, the shop seemed to do quite a good business in a bustling part of town, with people going in and out of its doors every day.

One day, a customer at the door inquired: "Is the owner in?"

In came a student of about twenty-seven or twenty-eight. Upon seeing the proprietor, he quickly produced a name card, asking: "Would you be Mr. Litman Deng?"

Looking at the card, the proprietor learned that the man's name was Tainted Fei. Tainted mentioned that he was eager to obtain material for a story competition at a certain daily newspaper.

"Of course!" Litman Deng replied eagerly. "You must be quite passionate about literature."

To his surprise, Tainted Fei replied: "Passionate? Hardly. I actually couldn't care less about it."

"But you would still have written quite a few pieces of fiction, I suppose," Litman ventured.

"Not at all," Tainted replied. "I don't even read the stuff, much less write it. Fiction is the most worthless form of literature—I detest it."

"If you dislike fiction so much," Litman asked in surprise, "why bother coming here for material?"

The other replied: "I'm hard up for ten dollars, so I want to write a story. Robbery or fiction-writing—it's one or the other if I'm going to put ten bucks in my pocket. Since robbery's illegal and fiction-writing isn't, I ..."

"Now wait a minute," Litman interrupted. "How can you lump fiction together with robbery? It's absurd! Literature is sacrosanct."

"Don't get angry, sir., Tainted hastily replied. "I'm just making an analogy. The truth is, I want to sit for this year's civil service examination.[1] I've prepared everything already, but registration requires a ten-dollar stamp tax, and the tuition allowance my family used to send me was cut off long ago. For good reason, I might add: my behavior used to be quite outrageous, so my relatives no longer trust me."

"I get it now," Litman said. "You want to write a story for this competition because you need ten dollars to pay the stamp tax."

Tainted clapped his hands in delight. "That's right! You're a quick one! Really, you're not just a man of letters; you've got the talent to be a magistrate."

Litman laughed. "Don't poke fun. Now, the fiction competition for that daily newspaper, is it for short stories?"

Tainted replied: "That's right—short stories of up to 5,000 words. That means that for less than 5,000 words you can get ten dollars. But that stamp tax really is a rip-off: *I'm* the one who has to write all these essays and yet it's still *me* who has to spend ten dol-

1. Up until the last few years of the Qing dynasty, government officials were selected through a three-tiered system of examinations, at the county, provincial, and national levels.

lars on stamps. If I don't pass, that's ten bucks down the drain, just like that. Isn't it ridiculous? It's exactly the opposite of writing fiction, and I get indignant just thinking about it."

Litman quickly responded: "You've got a point, but this is all a bit off topic."

Tainted nodded. "You're right. I shouldn't go off on a tangent. It's the same thing during the exam: if you go off on a tangent, you're bound to fail."

Litman drank a sip of tea and said, "In that case, listen while I tell you the story material:

"*The daughter of a poor family was in love with the son of an official. A neighbor's wife volunteered to act as matchmaker for her just as a joke, but the girl took her seriously and, as a consequence, ended up falling ill.*

"*The neighbor's wife reassured her, 'I'll ask the young man to visit you this evening. That'll relieve your illness.'*

"*Little did the girl expect that during the night the neighbor's wife would discuss the matter with her paramour, who later burst into the girl's room pretending to be the young man. In the dark the girl didn't have the strength to resist him, and she fell to the ground. The man snatched one of her embroidered shoes and ran off, only to drop the shoe en route. A butcher, seeing that the door to the neighbor's wife's house was open at night, snuck inside the house and his foot happened to land on the embroidered shoe, which he hid under his clothes. Eavesdropping from outside the room, the butcher overheard the paramour recounting to the neighbor's wife everything that had happened with the girl. The butcher then hurried over to the girl's house but entered her father's room by mistake. When the father yelled out, the butcher killed him and, in his panic to flee, dropped the embroidered shoe on the floor. In court, the girl had to confess that she had been visited by the young man, who was thrown in prison.*"

"Great! Great!" Tainted Fei exclaimed delightedly. "Although the girl had no intention of killing her father, her one fall from grace led to his death. This case really gives one a lot to chew on. At this point, I'd probably put the blame on the girl. Although the scenario is a bit contrived, if I can come up with an ingenious argument during the civil service examination to wow the examiners, I'm sure to pass. I've come across plenty of discussion topics of this sort: *A poisons B, but before B dies of poisoning, C kills B. Is A guilty?* Some said the murder was carried off, while others said it wasn't. I ruled not guilty, based on Article Two of the Penal Code. Ingenious, don't you think? Naturally, one *could* conclude that the crime was accomplished—you couldn't say that it wasn't because B died and A indirectly achieved his purpose. Then again, since it was achieved *indirectly*, his crime can only be labeled *attempted*. Furthermore, poisoning was not the cause of death. Thus, with regards to how to treat A's crime, the law is incomplete, not having foreseen this type of scenario. Now, as to the girl's crime ..."

"Hold on a minute," Litman interjected. "I wasn't bringing up a legal problem; I was only providing you story material."

Tainted Fei laughed. "I apologize. The material is great. So, I'll just need to write it down and then swap the manuscript for the reward money?"

"No guarantee. You can't be sure that you'll win." Litman replied.

"Of course I will!" Tainted responded. "The material is excellent, and it makes for an interesting legal problem too."

"The material may be good, but it's all in vain if the writing is poor."

"D'you mean to say that I can't just write down what you've told me and turn that in?"

"Exactly. Suppose you have a pound of pork: it's going to taste different if you cook it with vegetables or tofu, even though the raw material is the same."

"You've got a point!" Tainted exclaimed in surprise. "Is fiction writing as hard as all that?"

Litman replied: "If it were as easy as you seem to think, everyone would be a writer. Famous writers sometimes labor an entire day on just two or three lines. Others take the trouble to visit the places they write about before they put pen to paper. For example, one author who writes about conditions in the lower strata of society is celebrated for spending nights in the hovels of the poor."

Tainted laughed uproariously. "That's the stupidest thing I've ever heard of! As long as the main idea is entertaining, the writing itself is unimportant. You could put London in France or Mount Tai in the middle of the Atlantic Ocean and it wouldn't matter a bit. If you waste precious time over such petty details, how will literature ever prosper? In my view, literature of that sort will be the downfall of our country."

"Did you come here to attack literature, or did you come to get fiction material?" Litman asked, peeved.

"I didn't mean to offend you," Tainted said. "I came for material, and the stuff you told me just now was great. While you're at it, why not develop it into a story for me?"

Litman shook his head. "No. My job is providing the raw materials. You'll have to rely on your own abilities to polish it."

"In that case, I'll do it. Thanks!" With that, Tainted stood up and made to leave.

"Kindly pay for the material," Litman said anxiously.

"You mean it isn't free?"

"This is my profession," Litman replied. "How could I just give material away? I must charge ten percent of the estimated story value."

"A ten-percent cut!" Tainted exclaimed. "That's too expensive. I can get all kinds of material just listening to a storyteller spin tales of retribution, and that only costs thirty or forty cents."

"How can you liken my goods to that junk?" Litman responded in annoyance. "My materials are all first-class, nothing like that type of commodity."

"Can't you come down a bit?" Tainted asked. "How about this: I'm short on cash at the moment, so I'll pay for half now and settle up once I collect the prize money."

Litman said: "Literature isn't charity, but considering your situation, I won't insist. For the time being, we'll do as you suggest."

"Thanks for being so understanding, sir." Tainted replied. "If you were the examiner, we candidates would have it much easier."

So saying, he pulled a few coins from his pocket and placed them on the table.

## II

The second customer to enter the shop was a well-dressed young man of twenty-two or twenty-three. He exchanged a few words of greeting with Litman, who learned that his name was Handsome Xiao. Litman asked if he was here for story material, and the man replied that he had recently submitted manuscripts to several large bookshops.[2] Litman naturally responded by flattering him with a few compliments.

The man went on: "But those big bookshops would tell me that they had already accumulated stacks of manuscripts, and since they wouldn't be able to publish mine at the moment, they had to return it. So at this point I'm changing direction and trying for prize money in fiction-writing competitions."

Litman replied that he was sure to win.

"There was just one time ..." the man began.

"You won?" Litman interrupted.

"I was commended," the man said, "which is the same as not winning, so I'd be grateful if you'd help me come up with some new material."

"Excellent," Litman said. "What sort of material are you looking for?"

---

2. During the Republican era (1911–1949), bookshops often doubled as publishing houses.

"Courtesan fiction, ideally," Handsome replied, "and I have no need to conceal from you the reason for this. My friends lured me into the world of courtesans, and before long I couldn't live without them. There was one prostitute I wouldn't have given up even if it meant dying a horrible death, but my friends later informed me that she wasn't faithful to me—she actually had another lover. When I heard this, naturally I switched to a new courtesan. This one's great! She has the entire *Fiction Compendium* series displayed on a shelf in her room. Since she knows how to read and loves novels and short stories, everyone calls her the 'Literary Whore.' She fell head over heels for me when she found out I was a fiction writer. To be honest, none of us are willing to spend a cent to fool around with these women. It's only worthwhile if the woman pays our way."

"I see," Litman said. "And I take it you're writing fiction for the same reason?"

"That's right," Handsome replied. "She insists I write her a story, so I need to find some kind of virtuous prostitute-adventurer material. When she reads this story, she's sure to cherish me like her dearest treasure, and once her purse strings loosen I'll bring you a thank-you gift. I guarantee, once that story is finished, getting three of four lovers will be a piece of cake. What with royalties and allowances from my lovers—being a fiction writer is truly the best profession! Fiction is more effective than any aphrodisiac."

"You shouldn't talk about literature that way!" Litman exclaimed in annoyance. "But since providing materials is my job, obviously I can't refuse just because I don't like your motives. Alright then, here's your story material about a courtesan:

"*A young scholar and his friend were on their way to sit for the civil service examination, when they happened to stop in a brothel. The scholar fell in love at first sight with a prostitute and frittered away every last penny of his traveling expenses on whoring. Now empty-handed, he was in a fix. Suddenly, he remembered that his fiancée lived in the area, and that he might as well go borrow money for traveling expenses from his future father-in-law. Little did he know that his father-in-law was a snob. Seeing his son-in-law in such shabby clothing, he decided to renege on the marriage contract. Not only did he not lend the money, but he also forced the young man to sign a declaration breaking off the engagement before kicking him out of his house. When the virtuous and kindhearted fiancée received the letter, she committed suicide. The scholar, having been subjected to such extreme ignominy, was about to throw himself in the river, but just as he was about to jump, a woman in the window of an overlooking building spotted him and sent someone to stop him. The woman turned out to be the prostitute the scholar knew, and after he told her the reason for his distress, she provided him with money for traveling expenses to go sit for the examination. Later, after he had passed the exam and was on his way back, the father-in-law knew that trouble was brewing and figured out a way to acquire the prostitute and make her his adopted daughter. When the man returned to demand his bride, the father-in-law saved himself by marrying the prostitute to him, and the lovers were thus reunited."*

The tale no sooner finished than Handsome exclaimed: "Wonderful! She'll love it, and I'm sure to win the prize money. How much?"

Litman replied: "The rule here is to charge ten percent, so if we set the story's value at fifty dollars, the price would be five dollars."

"Five dollars?" Handsome asked. "How about three dollars for now?"

"Are you asking for a discount?" Litman asked.

"It's not that," Handsome replied. "I want to show it to her first and see how much I can get out of her, then I'll come pay the balance."

With this, he pulled out three dollar bills.

"I suppose that's how we'll have to do it," Litman said.

Having paid up, the man said goodbye and left.

## III

The next customer was a co-ed named Floozie Yang, who told Litman, "I submit new-style poems and the like to publications all the time, but they don't pay much, so I want to write fiction instead. You must have good material here, so I hope you'll let me have some."

"Absolutely!" Litman replied. "We have all types of story material here. I take it you're looking to make a name for yourself in the literary world?"

Floozie nodded.

"You're sure to become a famous female novelist." Litman assured her. "Besides, you're remarkably pretty. But that's enough of that. Tell me what you think of this material:

"*There once was a mean father who often maltreated his son. His daughter-in-law couldn't stand it, so she killed him. Having killed her father-in-law for the sake of her husband, she then killed herself.*

"Deep, wouldn't you say?"

"It's fine, but I'm looking for something purer," Floozie replied.

"Then how about if we follow the current fashion of discussing relationships between male and female students?"

Floozie nodded. "That's the only way to express modern consciousness."

"I've got it," Litman continued. "It's not in the very latest fashion, but it'll pass muster for another two or three years.

"*There was once a female student who was expelled from school for having had an affair with a male classmate. After the boy failed his examinations and the girl's family stopped sending her tuition money, the boy joined a gang of swindlers and often pressured the girl to hand over clothing and other possessions. Although the girl deeply regretted having met the boy in the first place, she was unwilling to break with him and gradually fell into dire straits."*

"That won't do!" Floozie exploded. "Don't you dare poke fun at us. How could you slander us like that?"

"What?" Litman asked in surprise. "I'm just providing story material, that's all."

"The nerve!" Floozie Yang went on. "Is my relationship with Mr. Tao any of your business? Our love is pure. We'll support each other until we grow old. Mr. Tao may not be in school anymore, but he's certainly never joined a gang of swindlers. Didn't he always get top grades in school? Doesn't a writer like you understand the sanctity of love? A wife shares in her husband's humiliation. Why are you insulting me?"

"You've got me wrong!" Litman protested. "It's a coincidence that the scenario I described resembles your circumstances. I would never insult you. Events like this happen all the time, and this story just happens to have some things in common with your situation."

"Their love is despicable, but ours is pure." Floozie declared. "I have to save Mr. Tao no matter what. There's no other way for me except for writing fiction and selling manuscripts. It's an act of devotion! I'm relying on you to choose good material for me. I want a good family drama."

"Here you go," Litman said.

"*A military officer engaged to a young woman was wounded in battle and ended up in a Red Cross hospital. The young woman served as nurse and took care of her fiancé. After he recovered, they married.*

"How does that sound?"

"Too plain," Floozie complained. "There are no waves."

"Let's make the waves billow, then," said Litman.

"*The young woman was in love with someone else who flew into a rage when he learned of her engagement. He happened to be a soldier too, and on the battlefield he shot the officer, who died of his wounds. The young woman was so distraught she wanted to end it all. She became an unshaven nun and every day visited his tomb to make offerings to his spirit. The soldier, still unable to attain his goal, repented of his error and committed suicide before the tomb.*"

Floozie shook her head. "Too tragic."

"Let's change it again, then," Litman said.

"*The officer was severely wounded, but the young woman did everything she could and ended up saving his life. Even so, he had lost both eyes and a foot. Although they could talk, he could never again see his beloved wife's smile.*"

"He'd be better off dead," Floozie said.

"Let him keep one eye, then," Litman suggested. "That way he'll be able to see. Or you could make him deaf. One set of materials can be modified at least ten different ways."

"Which option is best?" Floozie asked, "I can't decide."

Litman replied, "They're all about the same—all first-class goods. The price is the same too. I'd never sell you crude materials."

As the two were talking, a burly fellow came in and said to Litman: "I've already completed my manuscript, sir. Let me read it to you."

As he spoke, he took out a few sheets of paper.

Floozie Yang hurriedly interjected: "Let me go home and think about it. I'll come back and make a final decision tomorrow. Whatever you do, don't give these materials to anyone else."

With that, she said goodbye and left.

The burly man said: "I spent three days and nights thinking over the material you gave me before coming up with this piece. I've changed the meaning a bit, however, working in both our ideas. Let me read it to you."

## IV

"A short story should begin by describing scenery.

"*Outside the azure glazed window, red and white balsam—known as the 'phoenix immortal'—grew in scattered clusters, setting each other off in a pleasing contrast. A servant girl opened the window and bent over to pick flowers, which she placed in a slender-necked, wide-bodied vase. Evenly arranged, they looked quite attractive.*

"*The lady of the house had just woken up with nothing to do and was lazily finishing her morning toilette. Rubbing her sleepy eyes, she noticed the flowers and said to the servant girl: 'Last night while I was enjoying the cool air, I saw that the flower petals were still enclosed in buds, but today they've bloomed.'*

"*'That's right,' the servant girl answered with a smile. 'The flower and my lady both share the name of Phoenix. Last night's flower was as my lady was twenty days ago. This morning's flower resembles my lady of these past seven days.'*

"What do you think?"

"That's not right," Litman replied in annoyance. "Didn't the material I gave you have the moon as its theme? Why did you change it to a flower? The main character was named Moon too. How are you going to finish the story?"

"Now, just hold on a moment," the man said. "You don't realize that I don't have a moon story in me. I scratched my head for several days before settling on this flower story, so I made do with it. Listen to the rest:

"*This lady was a radiant beauty of eighteen or nineteen. Were a writer to describe her looks, he would tell of her limpid eyes, her soul as clear and cold as the autumn river, her figure as pure as jade, her face as rosy as a hibiscus flower, and her eyebrows as thin and arched as willow leaves. Or he would speak of her bright eyes and radiant white teeth, her cherry lips and slim waist. As Miss Phoenix sat beside her dressing table, her jade-white hand was about to gently open her toiletry case when she heard the servant girl's words.*

*"'Silly slave,' she said, pretending to glare at her. 'Who told you to go prattling on like that? Come here and comb my hair.'*

*"The servant girl stood behind Miss Phoenix to undo her bun and comb it out. After a moment, she spoke again: 'I've been here for a week now but never met the master. What does he look like? You said that the two of you were parted just half a month after you married. How could the master treat being apart so lightly?'"*

Litman waved his hand. "All wrong. In the material I gave you, the tragedy derived from it being a middle-aged nun speaking with an old woman. It's strange enough that you've made them younger. How could the nun also suddenly have a husband?"

The burly fellow listened to Litman, then, after staring blankly for a moment, said: "My story really isn't that clever. I'll just have to go back and rewrite it."

## V

The next customer who entered was a man in his forties, dressed in a dark gown with a skullcap slanted upon his head. Despite the cold, he carried a folding fan. He coughed to announce his presence and identified himself as Mr. Ma. After exchanging a few pleasantries, he looked around and commented on how well appointed the room was. In its center hung a six-foot scroll flanked by a pair of couplets inscribed by a famous hand. In the front of the room stood an ancient copper vase with a display of nandina and winter plum branches. At the back of the room, the grandfather clock chimed twelve. The mahogany furniture had been dusted clean and the windowpanes wiped spotless.

Bemused, Litman asked: "Are you here to buy story material?"

"Yes, yes, my apologies," the man replied, somewhat flustered. "I am obliged to entrust myself to the gentleman's kindness."

"What type of material are you looking for?" Litman asked.

"Everybody's sick of those old clichéd stories about secret

lovers' pacts made in the rear garden or the down-on-his-luck young man who takes first place in the civil service exam, so I'm looking for something new."

"Coming right up," Litman said.

"*There was a depraved girl who had affairs with two students simultaneously. Fortunately, she managed the situation with skill, hoodwinking both of them such that neither had a clue what was going on.*

"*One day, Student A told the girl: 'I need 1,000 dollars fast. If you really love me, please help me come up with something.'*

"*The girl hesitated for a moment, and then said: 'Leave it to me.'*

"*In fact, she already had a plan: Student B had repeatedly borrowed money from her to the tune of 1,000 dollars. The girl wanted the money back and had already pressed him several times, since she had her own debts to repay. Now with Student A entrusting her with this task on top of everything else, she pressed Student B as hard as possible. The funny thing was that the reason Student A was so anxious to get money was that he owed money to Student B. As the girl pressed Student B, he in turn pressed Student A, so that it became a circle of pressure. Student B, at a loss, was comforting the girl, when Student A unexpectedly happened to show up. When the three of them saw each other, everything became clear. The girl couldn't deceive them anymore, and the three were caught in an embarrassing situation.*

"How does that material sound?"

"Excellent!" the man replied. "It's sure to be popular."

"Do you intend to publish it in a magazine?" Litman asked.

The man shook his head. "No. I'm making a phonograph record—a storytelling ballad."

"You're not a writer?" Litman asked in surprise. "Are you a *tanci*[3] performer?"

---

3. A type of performing art with roots in Suzhou, consisting of storytelling with stringed accompaniment. Soaring Ma (Ma Rufei 馬如飛),

The man rapped his fan against the table and exclaimed: "See here! I am Soaring Ma's great-grandson. My name is Chicken Ma. I perform at the House of Uninhibited Joy."

"So that's it," Litman said. "No wonder you act so strange."

## VI

At that moment, in came a rich young man whose car was parked outside. Upon encountering Litman Deng, he didn't bother with "sir this" and "sir that," but spoke as if addressing the family accountant.

"Are you Deng?"

Litman told him his name with the utmost politeness, upon which he learned that this man was the scion of the eminent Zhu family.

"I came here especially to get story material," the man told him. "I've always been a great fan of literature."

He went on: "I do not write fiction for profit, nor do I engage in such base activities as competing for literary prizes. I plan to put out a single-volume book, but if it were sullied by the hands of a tradesman it would become vulgar and worthless, so I plan on publishing it myself. Once my book comes out, it naturally will garner considerable fame in society."

Litman remarked: "For your honor to condescend to write is already remarkable. That you would even do your own publishing is even more admirable. The printing and binding will no doubt be nothing but the best, and you'll surely 'make the price of paper rise in Luoyang,' astounding the world and leaving the doors of the bookshops deserted."

---

mentioned below, was a famous Suzhou *tanci* performer of the nineteenth century.

"What type of material do you have for me, then?" Master Zhu inquired.

Litman replied: "Choosing material for your honor is no trivial matter, so it's my duty to make a careful selection for you. Here you go:

"*There was a student endowed with both talent and good looks who sought a talented and beautiful wife. Yet he disdained the young ladies and society beauties he'd encountered, considering them all too vulgar. Instead, he fancied a certain prostitute, who was indeed endowed with talent and beauty. She too was in search of a talented and handsome husband, so each fulfilled the other's wishes. But how could a prostitute become a principal wife? To resolve this problem, the prostitute was willing to accept concubine status and search on his behalf for another young woman of talent and beauty who could serve as the principal wife. One rich household did have such a talented and beautiful daughter, but she had one flaw: she was by nature extremely jealous. Upon receiving the prostitute's letter, the girl thought of a strategy: she invited a group of literary men to a writing party as a means of choosing a husband. That day, the scholar was among the group, and as he was her target to begin with, he was, of course, chosen. They agreed to marry and move into the bride's household following the autumn examinations. The bride-to-be said to herself:*

"'*We'll see what that prostitute can do now that I'm the principal wife.*'

"*Little did she expect that this information would reach the ears of the prostitute, who, after searching for a long time, found yet another girl of consummate talent and beauty. Upon hearing of this, the prostitute prepared living quarters for her and, as soon as the autumn examinations concluded, welcomed the scholar into her chambers and saw to it that he married the other girl immediately. From then on, she locked the gate and forbade the groom from setting foot outside. At first, the rich family's daughter looked for her bridegroom but failed to find him. Later she realized that the other two had snatched him away, but all her efforts to get him back were in vain. Taking stock of the situation, she conceded defeat. She vowed to the two other wives that she would never be jealous again, and they all lived ... beautifully ever after.*

"This material should be good for two volumes and at least three hundred pages, if you work it right. Your honor's writing is sure to achieve an excellent reception in society."

"Good," Master Zhu said. "What is your price for these materials?"

Litman replied: "There's no standard price. Whatever your honor feels is appropriate."

"Shall we say a thousand dollars, then?" Master Zhu asked.

"No, no!" Litman exclaimed hastily. "Five hundred would be more than sufficient."

"I didn't bring cash with me today," Master Zhu told him, "so I'll have my chauffeur bring the money around later. When I've written my first draft, I'll come by again to discuss it with you. Sorry to have disturbed you."

He departed, leaving the dazed Litman feeling like he'd been possessed.

## VII

Ever since his shop opened, Litman Deng's business had prospered so much that he had considered opening branch stores in other major cities. One morning, he was visited by a bespectacled man in his thirties with a moustache shaped like an inverted "V" who referred to himself by his courtesy name, Swallowtail.

After the two had chatted for a while, Swallowtail asked: "How did you come to invent this new profession? Nowadays, novelties such as illustration studios and news bureaus providing materials to newspapers can be found everywhere, but what you've come up with is even more unique."

"Fiction has been all the rage in recent years," Litman replied. "Everybody's writing fiction. It's the only thing bookshop owners are interested in publishing, and readers of books and newspapers want to read nothing else. Even people with barely a passing knowledge of what fiction is all about—people with absolutely no conception of fiction or taste for the stuff—are going around writing and editing fiction. So fiction grows ever more abundant, even as it sinks deeper into crisis by the day. With demand outstripping supply, the content of published fiction has been drying up, all due to lack of material. I opened my shop to tackle this problem."

"You appear to be the only person in this line of work," Swallowtail remarked. "For one thing, no one has quite your breadth of knowledge. I myself came here today to ask you for some story material. I've come up with a few of my own ideas before but I never liked any of them. I'm looking for material for a short comic piece. Do you have anything that would suit?"

"Of course!" Litman replied. "Have a listen to this:

"*One winter evening, a man braved a blizzard to go knock on a doctor's door seeking medical help. The doctor was out, but a young boy opened the door and invited the man in, then said to him:*

"'*You came from the northeast riding a donkey that you borrowed from someone else. Your surname is Wang. The illness you are inquiring about is a difficult labor and the patient is your wife, am I right?*'

"*The man was shocked. 'You must be an immortal! How on earth did you guess? Please come quickly and make a diagnosis.'*

"'*No need,' the boy replied. 'Just return home and place one penny in the mother's hand and your son will be born.'*

"*The man returned home happily. The next day when the doctor returned and asked if any patients had come by yesterday, the boy recounted in detail the events of the previous evening. Hearing this, the doctor was infuriated and berated him: 'Are you crazy? What is this nonsense? How could you treat someone's life like a game?'*

"*The doctor grabbed a stick and was about to beat the boy when suddenly a group of people came in, exclaiming, 'Doctor, you are a true immortal!' as they bowed in thanks to the boy and showered him with gifts.*

*"The doctor was utterly mystified. As everyone was leaving he made a few inquiries and learned that they had followed the boy's instructions for dealing with a difficult labor, and that the baby had been born safe and sound. The doctor became even more perplexed and asked the boy to explain how all this had come about.*

*"The boy explained: 'I saw that the visitor's back had traces of snow and rain while there were none on the front, so I knew that he had come from the north. Seeing that his feet were not wet, I knew that he had ridden here on a donkey, and since he didn't lead the donkey into shelter, but left it standing in the snow and rain, I knew that it had been borrowed. Seeing the characters "Hall of the Three Scholartrees" on his bag, I knew that he was surnamed Wang ...'"*

As Litman reached this point, Swallowtail suddenly interrupted: "Wait a moment!

"*Emergencies are rare in winter, so he knew it was a difficult labor. The man looked worried, and he knew that he wouldn't unless it was his own wife.*

*"The doctor, still angry, persisted: 'And just where the heck did you hear that a penny could help induce delivery? Did you make that up?'*

*"'I didn't make it up,' the boy replied. 'In this world, money can make anything happen, even a baby's birth.'"*

Litman paled in amazement. "You know the story already?"

"Of course I do!" Swallowtail replied. "How could you give me this kind of material? This story was published previously in *Short Story Monthly*."

"I had no idea. It's probably a coincidence," the flustered Litman replied.

"A coincidence!? You're a fiction writer. How could you not know of Wofoshanren's[4] 'Doctor's Intuition'?"

As Litman was struggling for an answer, four or five people burst in—Tainted Fei, Handsome Xiao, and the others—and surrounded Litman Deng, all looking incensed. Litman was trapped.

Tainted Fei spoke first: "Just fine! What a rascal you turned out to be!"

Handsome Xiao chimed in: "Why are you bent on harming people like this?"

"What's the matter?" Litman asked.

Tainted Fei replied: "My story won first prize in the contest, sure enough, but when I went to collect the prize money, I found out that the material you gave me was pilfered! It came from the story "Rouge" in *Strange Tales from the Liao Studio*.[5] The judges discovered it immediately and the prize money was withdrawn. There's nothing else to say. Give me my deposit back!"

"You tricked me too!" Handsome complained. "When I turned your material into a story and showed it to my sweetheart, she laughed in my face, saying, 'I saw this before in an old issue of *Fiction Monthly*. The author is Cheng Dake. You have some nerve showing around a work you've plagiarized.' I'm so ashamed I can't bring myself to face her again."

"You got off easy," Tainted said. "Not only was my reputation tarnished, but I borrowed my deposit from friends. Just think what I've lost! I'm going to sue for sure."

"Gentlemen!" Swallowtail piped up. "His crime is truly unforgivable. On the other hand, each of you is engaged in writing yet you too seem to be guilty of negligence, since you aren't even fa-

4. A pen name of the famous late Qing writer Wu Woyao 吳沃堯 (1866–1910), also known as Wu Jianren 吳趼人.

5. *Liaozhai zhiyi* 聊齋志異 is a famous Qing dynasty collection of tales of the supernatural, written by Pu Songling 普松齡 (1640–1715). A selected translation by John Minford is available under the title *Strange Tales from a Chinese Studio* (Penguin Classics, 2006).

miliar with previously published stories. I suggest that you settle out of court. For starters, let's make him close shop."

With this, someone took down the shop sign.

"Gentlemen," Litman said tearfully, "things having come to such a pass, there's not much I can do. But my line of work is to supply materials wholesale, not to manufacture them myself. All wholesalers ever do is sell other people's ready-made goods. It's completely up to the buyer to determine whether or not the goods are new or used. If you like what you see, you buy it. As for plagiarizing, everybody nowadays is copying each other's works and rushing them to press. Why pick on me? Besides, I'm a promoter of Chinese goods. I never use foreign goods. Aren't those people who translate foreign fiction just plagiarizing? Why do you let them plagiarize and not me? Let's face it: fiction writers these days are a thick-skinned bunch, and copying old works is a trifle in comparison to what they're doing. Some people have the audacity to lift a passage here and a section there and piece them together into a comic story to trick readers. Isn't that even more absurd?"

*Zhuodai comments: Uh oh! This Litman Deng is on a tirade and might get around to cursing me. I dare not write another line, so it's time I lay down my pen.*

# The International Currency Reform Conference

I.M. Broke, reporter for *The Prospect*, was sitting by himself in the editorial office feeling bored. It was getting late. Some of his colleagues had already gone home, but even though he had no business of his own at the moment, he was obliged to wait. From his pocket he fished out and relit a half-smoked cigarette. A single drag seemed to take all his energy, and as he exhaled he tried hard to concentrate on savoring the flavor. In this age of runaway inflation, one couldn't even buy a cigarette without first counting one's coins!

He eased himself down into a rattan chair, but just as his mind was beginning to wander he heard sudden footsteps as someone rushed over to the doorway. Annoyed that someone had spoiled the comfortable atmosphere, he turned his head and saw a tea boy standing there, grinning at him.

"What do you want?" he bellowed. "What are you doing standing there smiling like that?"

The grinning tea boy was unfazed. "The director wants to see you."

Upon hearing the word "director," I.M. Broke scrambled to his feet and scurried over to the director's office. When calling on the director, of course, he adopted the demeanor of a subordinate having an audience with his superior and respectfully stood at attention to one side.

"I want you to go listen in on today's Reform Conference," the director told him, stroking his beard.

"What Reform Conference … ?" I.M. Broke asked hesitantly.

"You haven't heard about the Reform Conference?" the director asked in annoyance. "You're a reporter. How could you be so ignorant of current affairs? Didn't you know that special delegates from around the world are gathering here today for the International Currency Reform Conference? Get over there!"

With the director blowing up at him, I.M. Broke could only repeatedly nod his assent and withdraw. But he'd never heard of this Reform Conference—really! He hopped into a rickshaw and told the puller, "To the International Currency Reform Conference."

To his surprise, the rickshaw puller nodded and immediately set off. I.M. Broke thought to himself: *Here, even a rickshaw boy knows about the conference, while I, a bona fide reporter, haven't even heard of it. How humiliating!*

Just as an embarrassed I.M. Broke was breaking out in a cold sweat, the rickshaw pulled up in front of a large Western-style building. As he descended from the rickshaw he felt like a lost child, looking about aimlessly, but, sure enough, there above the door to the building was written in large letters: "International Currency Reform Conference." *This is the place, alright,* Broke nodded to himself. He hesitantly stepped inside and found himself in an enormous room already packed with people. It looked like the conference was about to begin. Unable to find a place to squeeze in, he went over to the media seats, where he was greeted by his fellow journalist, Joe Kerr, who waved him over with a laugh.

"Hey, Broke! What took you so long? The conference is starting."

I.M. Broke plunked himself down beside Joe Kerr, and asked him in surprise, "Even *you* knew about this conference?"

Joe Kerr burst out laughing, "You're kidding! Everyone in the world knows about this conference. You don't mean to tell me you only just found out about it? You've really got to get your act together! Listen and I'll tell you how this conference came about."

With that, he tossed aside his cigarette and began his story.

"You must know that after the end of the Great European War,[1] a World Reform Conference was held in Paris. At that time, the epidemic of inflation had infected the entire world, and every corner of the globe was packed with patients suffering its ill effects. Recent years were somewhat better, but lower-middle class people were hit hard, and things have now deteriorated considerably. Even rich aristocrats, high officials, and tycoons have found themselves in a precarious situation. How could the upper classes be feeling the pinch too? Because spiraling inflation has made the value of currency plummet. Worst off are national governments: their hands are tied and they can only watch the catastrophe unfold! In the past, a national government might only need a few billion dollars in spare change to get by, but now that's shot up to over a hundred billion. Governments have tried every means at their disposal, but most of their efforts have involved getting creative with taxation. We've had the sing-song girl drinking party tax, the brothel tea party tax, the transportation tax, the domestic servant tax, the bed tax, the clothing tax, the linens tax, the ring tax, the beard tax, the watch tax, the non-alcoholic beverage tax, the barber tax, the bath tax, the walking tax, the medicine tax, the eating tax, the pooping tax ... in short, everything's been taxed. It's easy to imagine what all this taxation has done to the impoverished, but now it's even pushed the rich into dire straits! Governments' last resort is to leave their citizens to starve to death. The problem is: if citizens starve to death, what kind of nation will be left? That would be unacceptable, so some of the world's clearer-headed people got together to discuss the issue. They concluded that the root cause of inflation was bad currency, and that we ought to abandon our flawed currency regime and switch to a new system that would free the people of the world from the oppression of

1. World War I (1914–1918).

money. Having reached this decision, they inaugurated this International Currency Reform Conference."

Joe Kerr concluded his voluble speech, leaving I.M. Broke stunned and temporarily at a loss for words.

A moment later, a bell sounded, signaling the start of the conference. The first person to take the podium was the Chinese special delegate, who had been elected chairman, Mr. Ngo Paw-wah. His face was gaunt with hunger, his frame as thin as kindling, and he delivered his opening remarks in the voice of a famine victim.

"Fellow delegates, today marks the opening of the International Currency Reform Conference. Due to rampant inflation, every country in the world has fallen on hard times. The cause of this calamity is none other than the cruel tyranny of currency fluctuation. Currency was originally created for the convenience and benefit of mankind, but things have recently gone wrong, and far from providing convenience, currency has enslaved the human race. Our use of currency has trapped us in a state of perpetual pain and suffering. Of all mankind's afflictions, poverty is the most worst. For mankind, currency has indeed been a sickness with no cure. Some men in the world may be unmoved by the charms of woman, but how many can resist the lure of gold? For ten grand, even a man hailed as the pride of a nation will resort to murder. The capitalist fattening himself on the blood and marrow of the working class, too, relies on money to acquire the privilege of riding in a motorcar. Driving down the boulevard against the flow of traffic, he makes pedestrians eat his dust, splashes them with mud, and fouls the air with his exhaust. If you don't meekly get out of his way, you face a death sentence—a trip straight to the guillotine. It boggles the mind! It's as if it's become a crime for poor people to walk on their own two feet! Nowadays, an individual's worth is judged solely by how much money he has. To command social respect, one has to live the gilded life. Without a doubt, money is a poison that will ruin society and vanquish mankind. We therefore call now for the death sentence for the vile, ruthless oppression of money!"

I.M. Broke was greatly moved by this speech. The next person to take the floor was the French delegate, Monsieur Misérable, whose sallow face was set on a long, thin neck.

"Mesdames et messieurs," he began bitterly, "the Great War has left every city and village in France completely devastated. Our once hale and hearty young men have all been transformed into cripples or invalids. Our funds have all been spent, leaving us penniless. The two things we have in abundance—conceited women and medals of valor—are utterly useless. Our nation might have gained the glorious title of victor, but glory is no substitute for bread to fill one's belly, nor can it serve as security for a loan. Our present situation, in short, is that we are starving to death as we anxiously wait for money to trickle in. The only way to relieve our poverty is to use other substitutes for our present currency. Your humble servant recommends that we replace currency with military medals and women. The value of medals could be fixed by type, on a scale from one to one hundred dollars. Women would be valued at one hundred to one thousand dollars based on age, physique, and other attributes. Should this resolution be adopted, I would hasten to begin continuous exports of this new currency, and import foreign foodstuffs into France to alleviate famine. This method would have the added advantages of checking recalcitrant warlords and preventing the expansion of the feminist and women's suffrage movements."

Monsieur Misérable's imaginative proposal was then followed by the German delegate, Herr Stonen-Broken, the British delegate, Mr. Skint, the Japanese delegate, Hongari-san, each of whom put forth brilliant proposals of their own.

Last came the American delegate, Mr. Pye N.D. Skye, who stood up and addressed attendees as follows: "I have the greatest admiration for my fellow delegates' esteemed views. Your humble servant's suggestion, however, is the simplest and easiest to implement, and could immediately alleviate social poverty. What, you ask, is this inspired plan? All that needs to be done is to invert the value of our currencies, such that a penny is worth one hundred dollars and a dime ten dollars. A ten-dollar bill would consequently become a dime and a hundred-dollar bill would become a penny. Should this method be accepted, a rich old man bestowing a hundred-dollar bill handout wouldn't raise an eyebrow, and the stacks of bills they keep in their safes at home would be worth next to nothing. At the same time, those thin and pallid commoners with no property except a handful of pennies would suddenly become well-to-do. The world would no longer be plagued by emaciated corpses, and all mankind would ring in a new age of peace."

This simple and ingenious proposition was immediately and unanimously approved. Happiest of all was I.M. Broke. Throughout his entire life, having a hundred dollars in his pocket had been no more than a fond fantasy. Now, all of a sudden, the pennies he knew so well were worth a hundred dollars each. How could he not be delirious with joy? Why, after buying a few cigarettes and paying for today's rickshaw, he still had four pennies in his pocket!

"As the owner of four precious pennies, I'm suddenly a man of modest fortune. Four hundred dollars! What better proof of this scheme's mind-blowing power to eradicate worldly misfortune? To begin with, I can escape this life of hardship. How wonderful! First thing I do, I'm gonna say goodbye to these old clothes and buy myself a couple of new outfits. Then I'll toss my two and a half months' of back rent in my landlord's face—see how he likes that! And I won't have to listen to my wife complaining at the end of each month any more. Hip hip hooray! The world's become a paradise!"

With these happy thoughts, I.M. Broke couldn't help dancing for joy.

* * *

A typesetter bringing proofs to the editorial office was greeted by the sight of I.M. Broke still sleeping in the rattan recliner, his arms and legs flailing about wildly.

"Wake up, Mr. Broke!" he called out. "With the price of everything going up so fast, just think what a disaster it would be if you caught cold!"

# Plagiarist in Western Dress

Dear Readers:

Just who, do you suppose, is this plagiarist in Western dress? None other than yours truly. Those of you who know me personally or have seen my photograph will say, "That's right—you do tend to wear a Western suit, but I have no idea which story you plagiarized." To this, I reply, "I plagiarized the one you're reading right now." And just why would I plagiarize a short story? I must pin the blame on the editor of this magazine, my buddy Shi Jiqun.[1] It's like this: the day before yesterday, Jiqun came over to my house to discuss the massive problems he faces in processing manuscript submissions. Besides the manuscripts he receives from a few close friends, he also receives a large volume of submissions from the general public. Many of these are excellent, and our magazine publishes the best ones immediately in order to promote emerging talents. Once a work appears in print, however, we're often surprised to receive a letter from someone claiming that the piece was plagiarized from somewhere or other. Dangers abound! After all, it's impossible for a person screening manuscripts to have read *every single* work of fiction out there! Some unforgiving readers even

1. Shi Jiqun 施濟群 (1896–1946) was a prolific editor and writer of popular fiction (especially detective and comic fiction) who worked closely with Xu Zhuodai at *The Scarlet Magazine* and other periodicals during the 1920s.

accuse us of having ourselves plagiarized works to make up our publishing quota. This is why Shi Jiqun has to review unsolicited manuscripts with the greatest care, and why he asks old friends to write extra pieces.

After Mr. Shi left, I was suddenly struck by a funny thought. *He's gotten too trusting*, I said to myself. *Does he really believe that his old pals won't throw a monkey wrench in the works by submitting a plagiarized piece of their own? Are we that reliable?* Since he trusts me so implicitly, if I happened to plagiarize something he might not detect it. That way I could try out my as-yet-untested special plagiarizing technique and dupe everyone. Even readers wouldn't be able to tell that the story's plagiarized. What would I have to lose? That said, I mean it when I say that I don't want my editor or readers to be able to detect my plagiarism. My special plagiarizing technique can pull the wool over everyone's eyes, so I have nothing to fear. It's extremely effective, and I've only just invented it, so who will be the wiser? This fact makes me even bolder and my skin even thicker, so I'll give it to my editor and readers straight: this story you're about to read is plagiarized. The key thing is this: my method is so novel that you'll never be able to identify the source text, and it'll read like an original work. I can't be stopped! Having given due notice to everyone up front, I'm going to skip the niceties, put pen to paper, and start plagiarizing right away.

* * *

When George was out, his black slave girls had the run of his quarters and availed themselves of his absence by amusing themselves as they saw fit. Some played ping-pong, while others played poker, and the floor was soon strewn with cigarette butts. Unfortunately, just then the old wet nurse Mrs. John came in, leaning on her walking stick, to pay George a visit. Finding George out and the black slave girls goofing off, Mrs. John was highly displeased.

"Ever since I moved out and stopped coming by so often, you girls have been getting more and more out of line, and the other nannies have been unwilling to take you to task. That George is like a three-hundred-meter lighthouse: he can see other people clearly but can't see himself. He's always complaining about how messy other people are, but just look at the mess you've made of his room!"

The slave girls were well aware that George was not overly concerned about tidiness. Moreover, Mrs. John had been pensioned off and had no more authority over them, so they just smiled and ignored her. Yet Mrs. John continued to press them about such matters as how many pieces of bread George ate at mealtimes and what time he went to bed. To each query, the black slave girls responded with some facetious answer.

"Horrid old bag!" one exclaimed.

Mrs. John then asked, "Why haven't you offered me this glass of brandy?"

So saying, she picked it up and began to drink.

"Stop!" one black slave girl interjected. "George was saving that for Melina. If he gets back and discovers that you drank it, he'll be angry and you'll have to admit that you did this of your own accord—don't make us take the blame!"

Mrs. John felt angry and humiliated.

"I refuse to believe that he'd suddenly be so inconsiderate. What's one glass of brandy? He shouldn't begrudge me even if it was something far more expensive. Do you imagine that Melina means more to him than I do? Has he forgotten who brought him up? The milk he grew up drinking flowed from the blood in my veins. Is he going to get mad at me for drinking a single glass of brandy? I'm going to drink it, and we'll just see what he does! You see that Melina stays out of this. I trained that little imp of a maid myself. Who's she to me?"

With that, she haughtily downed the glass of brandy.

Another black slave girl laughed.

"They shouldn't say things to get under your skin like that, ma'am. George will surely send you gifts to convey his filial respect. He wouldn't get worked up over a thing like this."

"Don't waste your breath trying to flatter me," Mrs. John replied. "Do you think I don't know about the earlier incident when Jean was dismissed over the coffee? If there's a problem tomorrow, I'll return to face the music."

With that, she stormed off.

A short while later George returned and sent for Melina. Seeing Micky collapsed on the sofa, George asked, "Are you sick, or did you lose the game?"

"She was winning all right," Sheila said, "but when Mrs. John came by just now she messed up and lost. She got so mad she fell asleep."

George laughed. "Don't let that old fuddy-duddy bother you."

Just then, Melina arrived. Seeing George, she asked him where he had gone to eat and when he had returned. She also passed along her mother's regards to the other black slave girls, and then took a moment to change into a more casual outfit.

George ordered the brandy brought over, but the black slave girls told him that Mrs. John had drunk it. George was about to say something when Melina cut in with a smile, "So you were saving it for me—thank you so much! Last time I had brandy I enjoyed it while I was drinking it, but then I got a bad stomachache afterwards, one so bad that I didn't feel better until I had thrown up. It's just as well that she drank it; otherwise it'd have gone to waste. I'd prefer to eat a chocolate bar. Unwrap one for me while I go make the bed."

George took her at her word, and after putting the brandy away he brought out a chocolate bar and unwrapped it under the light of the electric lamp. Seeing that the others had left the room he smiled at Melina.

"Who was that wearing red today?"

"That was my second younger cousin," Melina replied.

Hearing this, George let out a couple of sighs.

"What are you sighing about?" Melina asked. "I know what's on your mind: you're going to say that she doesn't look good in red."

George laughed. "No, no. If someone like her couldn't wear red, who could? I was just thinking how nice she is and how wonderful it would be if she were in our household."

Melina smiled sardonically. "Isn't it enough that I alone have to suffer the fate of a slave? Do all my family members have to experience the same? Why do you have to pick all the best maids to come live in your house?"

Hearing this, George quickly responded with a smile. "You're overreacting again. Did I say that everybody who comes to this house has to be a slave? What's wrong with just a 'relative'?"

"She would make an unworthy marriage partner for you," Melina replied.

George was unwilling to continue this exchange and went back to unwrapping the chocolate bar.

Melina laughed. "Why won't you talk? My impertinence just now must have given you a shock. Tomorrow, why don't you just spend several hundred pounds sterling and buy her for spite?"

George smiled. "How am I supposed to respond to that? I just meant that I liked her and that it's she who should have been born into a grand mansion like this one, instead of insensitive creatures like those of us who actually were."

"She didn't enjoy such good fortune, but her parents doted on her. She's seventeen and the apple of my maternal aunt and uncle's eyes. They've already prepared a generous dowry for her, and she's to be married off next year."

Hearing the words "married off," George couldn't suppress another couple of breathless exclamations.

Feeling out of sorts, Melina sighed again. "In the few years I've been here I haven't been able to be together with my sisters. Now that I'm going back home, they've all left."

George detected that she was hinting at something and dropped the chocolate bar in surprise.

"What do you mean you're going back home?" he hurriedly asked.

Melina told him, “Today I heard my mom and my elder brother discussing how they plan to have me stick it out one more year, and that they’ll return next year to buy me out of service.”

Hearing this, George grew even more agitated.

“Why do they want to buy your freedom?”

“What a strange question!” Melina replied. “I’m not some flesh-and-blood relation of your family. My family all lives elsewhere; am I supposed to live here alone forever?”

“It would be hard for me to force you to stay, then,” George said.

“That’s not the way things are done,” Melina replied. “Even in the imperial palace the standing rule is that slaves only stay for a few years—never indefinitely. Your household is no exception.”

George pondered for a moment and then accepted this wisdom.

“It would be difficult for my grandmother not to release you from service either.”

“Why wouldn’t she release me?” Melina asked. “Perhaps if I was a rare treasure. Or maybe if I struck a chord with your grandmother and mother and they didn’t have to let me go because they found a way to come up with several hundred pounds sterling to keep me here. If so, that might be possible. But in fact I’m only an ordinary maid; there are plenty of people better than me. I’ve been in your grandmother’s care since I was a girl. I served Miss Lea for the first few years, and I’ve been serving you now for several years too. It’s only right that my family come to redeem me now. Out of kindness, they might even let me go without asking for the redemption money. They wouldn’t refuse to let my family redeem me just because you say I’ve served you well. I’ve done just as I should as a member of your household. I haven’t rendered any particularly meritorious service. You’ll still have other good people to look after you after I go. It’s not like you won’t be able to do without me.”

George became even more agitated, having heard innumerable reasons why she should go but none why she should stay.

"That may be the case, but I'm set on keeping you here. Don't worry, I'll have Grandmother speak to your mother. If we give your mother enough pounds sterling, she'd be too embarrassed to take you away."

Melina replied, "Of course my mother wouldn't insist, but you'd have to break it to her gently. It wouldn't be good to tell her that you're going to give her extra money. If, on the other hand, you told her that you were going to hold me here without giving her a penny she wouldn't dare object, but your family has never been in the habit of acting in such a high-handed manner. To do so would be even worse than to buy something for ten times the market price—how fair would that be to the seller? How would you be any different if you retained me for no reason, keeping me apart from my flesh and blood? Your grandmother and my mother would never agree to it."

George thought about this for a moment and then remarked, "From everything you've said, it sounds like you're going for sure."

"For sure," Melina confirmed.

George thought to himself: "Who would have thought that a treasure like her could be so heartless?"

He then said with a sigh, "If I had known before that you were going to leave me a lonely ghost like this, I would never have let you come here in the first place."

With that, he angrily got into bed and went to sleep.

In fact, when Melina was at home and had overheard her mother's plans to buy her freedom and bring her back home, she had told her she'd rather kill herself than go home. Moreover, she'd told her mother, "Back then the family didn't even have bread to eat. All you had was me, who was still worth several hundred pounds sterling, and I told you to sell me because I was unwilling to watch my father starve to death. Now I've been fortunate enough to be sold into a good family where I eat and dress as well as my masters, who never beat me or curse me. Moreover, even though dad's gone now, our branch of the family has regained its status and vitality. You shouldn't bring hardship upon yourselves by begging or borrowing money to buy my freedom, and there's no need to anyway. Why do you want to buy my freedom anyway? Just pretend I'm dead and drop the idea of buying my freedom."

Seeing her cry and raise such a fuss, her mother and elder brother realized that she was determined never to leave that household. Furthermore, she had been sold to George's family for life. They were dependent on his family's benevolence, and if they did ask to redeem Melina, George's family might well return her without demanding repayment. Second, George's family never mistreated their servants; they were generous and unpretentious. Further, the girls who waited on the members of that family—no matter whether they served the elder or younger generation—all enjoyed higher status than those working for other families. Even unattached daughters from poorer households did not command as much respect. As such, Melina's mother and brother abandoned the idea of buying her out of servitude. Later, when George suddenly departed, given their situation, things became clearer for the two of them, and they felt like a rock had been lifted off their chests. Hoping for the best, they relaxed and let the matter drop.

But let us return to Melina, who had observed George's unusual personality since childhood. He had been much more naughty and mischievous than the other children, and exhibited a number of eccentricities that were hard to put into words. Recently, because his grandmother doted on him and because his parents were unable to keep a tight rein on him, he had become even more out of control and willful. He was unwilling to take on any real responsibilities and stubbornly unresponsive to any entreaties. As such, in bringing up the matter of buying her freedom Melina had intentionally tricked him by playing on his emotions to keep him from getting angry. Sure enough, George had gone to bed without saying anything. She knew that he was overcome by emotion and was now feeling down in the dumps. She hadn't really wanted to eat a chocolate bar in the first place, but she'd pretended she did in order to prevent an incident over the brandy like the one with Jean and the coffee. The danger had passed when George didn't bring it up, so she ordered the slave girls to take the chocolate bar away and eat it themselves. She went over and gave George a nudge and saw that his face was streaming with tears.

Melina smiled. "What's worth getting so sad about? If you really want to keep me, of course I won't go."

Catching on, George said, "Given everything you just said, how can I keep you? Even I can't come up with a reason."

Melina smiled. "We've always gotten along well; that's not an issue. But if it's really you who wants to keep me and not just your elders, I want you to agree to three requests. If you agree to my wishes, that'll mean you really do want to keep me, in which case I wouldn't leave even if someone held a gun to my head."

George hurriedly smiled and said, "I'll agree to any request you make, my dear, dear sister! Even if you made two hundred or three hundred requests instead of just three, I'd agree to them all. I only ask that you watch over me and take care of me until the day that I turn to dust—or never mind dust, which has tangible form and carries memories—instead, wait till I turn into a wisp of smoke and disappear in a puff of air. When that happens, all of you maids won't be responsible for me anymore, and I won't have to worry about you all anymore either. When I'm gone, you can all go wherever you like."

Seeing his state of agitation, Melina interrupted, "All right, all right! So I was a little mean in making my case."

George hurriedly replied, "Say no more!"

* * *

Jiqun remarks: So my old buddy is a plagiarist—I never knew! My apologies for failing to pay you due respect! This story, as far as I can see, is clearly a translation. I dare not suggest that my old buddy plagiarized it. Some places in the story are underlined in black. These are names of foreigners and foreign objects, which we specially marked to prevent reader confusion. Zhuodai, old buddy, since you confess to being a plagiarist, I suggest you come clean. How about you make an announcement in the next issue?

# Addendum: Expose Plagiarism!

Dear Readers:

In the previous issue I published a love story about a young playboy, George, and his black slave girl, Melina, in the hopes that I could dupe Mr. Shi Jiqun. Little did I expect that he'd see through me right away and even underline in black disparities between my version and the original. As you can see, the non-underlined parts were completely plagiarized. And if that weren't enough, he's making me come clean too. At this point, since he's seen through me, the only thing left for me to do is to bite the bullet and write my confession.

The first thing I want to announce is that this story was indeed plagiarized—not translated. Nor was the source text from which I plagiarized it a translation either; it was a Chinese work. Nor is the source text some piece published in an obscure magazine or the newspaper. It's an immensely famous novel that every single reader of fiction will have heard of. Thanks to my foolproof technique, however, none of you have been able to trace its origins. If you still haven't identified the source text, I'd be more than happy to help you. I present, with my compliments, a dictionary for the reader's reference.

## A SMALL DICTIONARY FOR THE EXPOSURE OF PLAGIARISTS

| | |
|---|---|
| George | Baoyu |
| ping-pong | Chinese chess [*go*] |
| play poker | play Racing Go and Dice and Dominos |
| cigarette butts | melon seed shells |
| Mrs. John | Nannie Li |
| walking stick | cane |
| black slave girls | maids |
| three-hundred-meter lighthouse | six-foot lampstand |
| bread | rice |
| brandy | koumiss |
| Melina | Aroma |
| coffee | tea |
| Jean | Snowpink |
| Micky | Skybright |
| sofa | bed |
| Sheila | Ripple |
| chocolate bar | dried chestnuts |
| fate of a slave | slave's fate |
| several hundred pounds sterling | several taels of silver |
| Miss Lea | Miss Shi |
| gun | knife |

Dear Readers:

With this dictionary in hand, you've been able to figure it out, haven't you?[1] Is my plagiarizing method impressive or what? When plagiarizing, I used this dictionary to reclothe the story in foreign dress; without it, you'd be clueless! I've insured myself with a foreign insurance company, hired a foreign lawyer on long-term retainer, and slapped a foreign brand on my product. Am I going to worry about anybody trying to sue me? I might as up and tell you: this "foreign dress" plagiarizing technique wasn't my own invention either—I plagiarized that too! Haven't you seen? Most of the jokes appearing in newspapers and magazines in recent years have been stale ones. Writers will take *The Expanded Forest of Laughs*, for instance, and change a "school teacher" into a "coach" and call it a new joke, or change "Mrs. So-and-so" into "Mr. Smith's mother" and pass it off as a Western joke. I'm just ripping off their technique. Should there be any aspiring plagiarists out there, let me recommend my "foreign dress" plagiarizing technique—it's safe as houses.

1. See Cao Xueqin, *The Story of the Stone: Volume I*. Tr. David Hawkes (London and New York: Penguin Classics, 1973), pp. 383–392.

# The Unofficial Stories of Li Ah Mao

## A. APRIL FOOL'S DAY

The newlyweds usually passed their evenings quietly in the living room. Today, however, an earth-shaking fight broke out.

A letter had arrived addressed to the husband, and when the wife opened it she'd discovered it was a love letter from a woman, and an extremely sappy one at that.

Naturally, when her husband returned home all hell broke loose.

WIFE: I never thought that you were this kind of man! I married you because I trusted you completely, but it turns out I was duped!

The letter still lay on the table as incontrovertible proof. The husband went red-faced and stayed silent when faced with the damning evidence.

WIFE: You're a good man in other respects, but you have something of a roving eye. (*Weeping.*) You're so easily corrupted! (*Bawling.*) I completely misjudged you. If I had known you were like this, I'd never have married you!

The husband kept his peace, knowing that it would be counterproductive for him to open his mouth. To do so would only give

his wife more material to use against him. At any rate, it was the girl's fault. Why did she mail the letter to his house?

Wife: I wouldn't complain if the girl was the daughter of some renowned family, but she's a *waitress* of all things. (*Cries.*) I never should have married a fool like you! (*Cries again.*) I won't stay here a minute longer. (*Turning angry.*) I want out—I'm leaving!

Husband: (*Losing his temper.*) Get out! Get the hell out!

Wife: (*Enraged.*) Fine! I'm leaving, I'm leaving.

Having said this, she bursts into tears. But a moment later she suddenly sits down.

Wife: I'm not going anywhere. I can't go back to my parents' house, having already married you good and proper. And besides my parents' house, were else do I have to go? Death is my only option!

Her husband is momentarily shocked but retains his composure.

HUSBAND: Now *that's* interesting!

WIFE: *What's* interesting? I saw this day coming long ago.

HUSBAND: What foresight—what rare brilliance!

WIFE: I've made my preparations. I bought two bottles of sleeping pills and I can turn on the gas any time. I even hammered a nail into the ceiling over our headboard so that I can hang myself.

HUSBAND: If you're going to kill yourself then kill yourself. Once is more than enough.

WIFE: I'm conscientious in everything I do. First I'll take the sleeping pills, then I'll turn on the gas, and finally I'll hang myself. I'll be a goner for sure!

HUSBAND: "If your will is set, you're sure to succeed." Get on with it then!

WIFE: I will—just watch me.

The wife suddenly stands up, and her husband starts to panic in spite of himself.

At that very moment, a man walks in the front door.

VISITOR: Pardon me.

The couple looks and sees a forty-something-year-old man carrying a leather briefcase, who gives the appearance of a visitor from overseas.

HUSBAND: Who is this?

The visitor stands silently by the window.

HUSBAND: Who are you? (*Looks back at his wife.*) Is he a relative of yours from home?

The wife examines the man closely.

WIFE: He's no one I know!

HUSBAND: What do you want? I'm afraid you've come to the wrong house.

The visitor looks blankly at the couple and then suddenly bursts into a wail—the living picture of a naughty child.

The husband and wife jump in surprise.

Wife: What's wrong?

The visitor continues crying for a while before replying:

Visitor: Yes, it's this house and no mistake. Four years ago in this very living room, I …

Without finishing, he begins bawling again.

Wife: What is it? Why are you crying in our house?

Visitor: I'm sorry! I'm sorry! I must have given you a shock. I used to live in this house, and four years ago my wife died in this very room. It was all my fault: I had an affair and quarreled with my wife, who then turned on the gas and committed suicide.

Husband and wife stare at each other, their hearts skipping a beat.

VISITOR: I came here because today is the fourth anniversary of her passing. My sincere apologies! Would you permit me to offer a prayer in this room?

The couple is momentarily at a loss for words.

VISITOR: My wife died a wrongful death and might haunt this house or attempt to transmigrate her spirit into a new body. It would be better if I said a prayer.

So saying, he walks into the middle of the room with his briefcase.

VISITOR: Ai! It looks about the same as four years ago. Her corpse lay over here on the east side of the room. (*He starts crying again.*)

Hearing this, the husband and wife become frightened.

VISITOR: I'm so sorry to impose on you! Would you mind giving me a moment alone in the room to say a prayer?
WIFE: Fine! Fine! We'll go to the atrium.
HUSBAND: Goodness! What a pity.

The couple walk into the atrium and open the window, through which they can hear the man murmuring his prayer.

VISITOR: Our Savior says, "I am the resurrection and the life. He who believes in Me, though he may die, he shall live. And whoever lives and believes in Me shall never die."

From the atrium, the couple hang on every word.

VISITOR: Oh, omnipotent Heavenly Lord! I entrust the soul of my deceased wife to you, Lord. We have faith in our Lord Jesus Christ and firmly believe that His followers will be resurrected in glory and enjoy eternal life. Come Judgment Day, our Lord Jesus Christ, in all His awe-inspiring glory, will appear during the Second Coming to pass His judgment on the people of the world. At that time, the dead in the earth and the sea will arise, and our Lord Jesus will use His great power to restore all beings to His embrace, transforming the decayed bodies of Christians at rest into glorious bodies like His own. Amen!

Having listened to the man finish his prayer, the couple see him pick up his suitcase and walk out.

VISITOR: My sincere thanks! You've let me set things right with her. Goodbye, goodbye.

WIFE: So his wife killed herself by leaving the gas on. How frightening!

The two walk into the living room.

WIFE: Aiya! The cuckoo clock and the thermos have disappeared!

HUSBAND: Something's wrong! My wallet's gone too. Oh no—we've been tricked!

With this, the husband races out in pursuit. The wife then notices the date on the calendar—April 1st—and, beside the calendar, a calling card with three words on it: "Li Ah Mao."

* * *

## B. TURNED AROUND

"Would you be Mr. Li?"

Big Wang opened the door and saw standing before him in the moonlight a fat man in a Western suit carrying a briefcase.

The fat man nodded. "That's right. Did Little Zhou already inform you of my visit?"

"Yes, he did, Mr. Li. He had someone deliver the message in person this afternoon. Please come in and have a seat!"

Li Ah Mao stepped inside and Big Wang closed the door behind him. The two walked through a small courtyard. Big Wang's house was just three small rooms. As they walked into the middle room Li Ah Mao saw in the dim lamplight a coffin lying in the middle of the room.

"Please have a seat. My apologies for the cramped quarters."

Ah Mao sat down on a bamboo chair.

"Today Mr. Zhou sent someone to tell me that a Mr. Li was coming to our village to stay for a few days. Naturally, since Mr. Li is Mr. Zhou's friend, I'll do my best to look after him. The only thing is that I have just these three rooms. The left one is where I sleep with my wife, who gave birth to a child three days ago."

As he spoke, Big Wang helped Li Ah Mao from his chair and led him into the room on the right-hand side.

"This is our kitchen. We also keep a few pigs here and use the room for storage ..."

They returned to the middle room.

"... so I can only invite Mr. Li to sleep in this room. I'll have my brother set up bedding for you, but the coffin will be here. It's my mother, who passed away less than a hundred days ago.[2] Mr. Li, I must apologize for this inconvenience."

---

2. The traditional period of mourning for a Chinese family was one hundred days. The open coffin of the deceased would be kept in the house for forty-nine days, with prayer ceremonies held every seven days. The coffin would then be sealed and interred.

"Not at all! Everything's fine."

Li Ah Mao looked at the altar and saw an inscription on the ancestral tablet: "Lady of the Wang Household, *née* Zhang."

"Mr. Li! I'm worried that you'll be afraid to sleep next to a coffin. After all, it is a bit unusual, isn't it? I've asked my younger brother, Lao Er, to keep you company at night by pounding rice in the next room. This way you can have a good, relaxing sleep."

Big Wang paused.

"Mr. Li, have you had supper yet?"

"I ate on the road."

"In that case, you can turn in early."

With that, Big Wang had his brother Lao Er come in and lay out the bedding, after which he himself prepared a teapot, matches, and the like. Before long, everything was ready.

"Get some rest, Mr. Li! If you need anything, don't hesitate to ask my brother; he'll be up all night."

With a bow, Big Wang excused himself and went back to his own room, while Lao Er began pounding rice in the room next door. Pigs could be heard snuffling in the background. Li Ah Mao changed clothes and got into bed. Though he was in a new place, he was so exhausted from his journey that he fell right asleep.

By the time Li Ah Mao awoke from his slumber it was already late morning, and he could hear the brothers having a conversation.

"This mortar wasn't set up correctly, so pounding rice has been more laborious than it should be," Lao Er was saying.

"It was just set up so it'll probably take you more than a day to get used to it, don't you think?" Big Wang replied.

Li Ah Mao dressed and got up. Big Wang heard him and came over.

"Good morning, Mr. Li! Did you sleep well last night?"

"Extremely well!"

"Wonderful. I was worried that sleeping next to a coffin you'd be afraid ..."

As Big Wang spoke he looked over at the altar and suddenly cried out in alarm:

"Aiya!"

Lao Er heard him yell and came over.

"What is it?"

"Look! The ancestral tablet!"

They looked at the ancestral tablet on the altar and a bizarre sight greeted their eyes. The tablet had been facing the doorway yesterday evening, but this morning it had turned so that its back faced the door. In one night, it had turned completely around. How bizarre!

"Mr. Li, did you move it?"

"No!" Li Ah Mao shook his head. "I just got up and hadn't even noticed it."

"What could it be?"

"Could mom be haunting us?"

"Now why would she want to do that? She hasn't haunted us in the three months since she died. Why would she suddenly haunt us now?"

"Think about it! The bier was here when your wife was giving birth in the next room. The blood must have offended her!"

"Could it be …?"

All three were utterly mystified. Big Wang quickly lit three sticks of incense and kowtowed three times before turning the tablet back around to its proper direction. He then prepared a basin for Li Ah Mao to wash his face.

That day Li Ah Mao was out working all day and didn't come back until late at night. After exchanging a few words with the elder Wang he went straight to bed.

Just before falling asleep, he took a good look at the self-revolving tablet and couldn't help feeling a little scared. That night, Lao Er again kept him company by pounding rice.

Li Ah Mao woke up the next morning and sat up to take a look at the ancestral tablet.

"Aiya! It turned around again."

Hearing this, the brothers hurried in and were struck dumb by what they saw.

"Has something like this ever happened before?"

"No, never!"

"What a curious problem! I've got to get to the bottom of this."

The two brothers were shaken up, but Li Ah Mao kept his cool. That day he went out as before and returned at dusk.

The younger Wang had slept during the day and kept Li Ah Mao company at night by pounding rice.

On the third night, Li Ah Mao suddenly woke up at midnight and heard Lao Er thump, thump, thumping away as usual in the other room. He sat up quietly, struck a match, and looked at the tablet. Oddly, it had moved again but this time counterclockwise instead of clockwise.

Instead of alarming Lao Er, Li Ah Mao reached over to the tablet, turned it back around to its proper place, and then went back to sleep.

The next morning before Li Ah Mao had woken up, the Wang brothers were already exclaiming in surprise in front of the altar. When he awoke, Ah Mao saw that the tablet had turned counter clockwise just like last night. Instead of explaining that he had moved the tablet the night before, he just looked at it and smiled.

"Don't worry, you two! Tonight the tablet likely won't spin around again."

"Why?"

"I'll tell you tomorrow."

That night, Li Ah Mao told Lao Er, "The sound of the rice-pounding is actually keeping me up at night. Why don't you take the night off?"

Accordingly, Lao Er went off to sleep in the pig pen.

First thing the next morning, everyone went to look at the tablet. And strangely, just as Ah Mao had predicted, the tablet hadn't moved an inch. There it was, facing the doorway.

"Mr. Li! How do you explain this?"

"The tablet never was able to move on its own. Rice-pounding in the new mortar shook the tablet so that it revolved in small increments. Over the course of a night it turned exactly 180 degrees. The night before last Lao Er pounded for an entire night but the tablet only turned ninety degrees. Actually, I had woken up at midnight, seen that it had turned counterclockwise, and turned it back to its original place. By the next morning it had turned another ninety degrees, which adds up to 180 degrees. To tell the truth, it was that ninety degrees that helped me solve this mystery. Ha ha!"

* * *

## C. THE MARKETING DIRECTOR

"The wise businessman never has to spend extra on advertising in order to expand his business."

Eminent Li,[3] the newly hired Marketing Director for Culture Books sitting opposite Manager Feng, went on:

"The clever industrialist, for instance, is able to make useful products out of cheap raw materials or raw materials that others have discarded. This is the only way one's enterprise will succeed. It's no different for us businessmen, but of course you'll have no business unless you advertise. That said, it makes no sense to spend too much on promotion."

"Right! You're absolutely right!" Manager Feng nodded. "Advertising these days costs an arm and a leg. How on earth are we supposed to advertise?"

---

3. Mr. Li's given name, Gongding 公鼎 literally means "esteemed by the public." *Ding* 鼎 can also refer to a type of ancient bronze cooking vessel.

"That's why we'd be best off availing ourselves of opportunities for free advertising."

"Is there such thing as free advertising?" The manager didn't understand.

"There are plenty of would-be volunteer advertisers out there. We just need to be able to identify them in order to make use of them."

"But no one would willingly be a volunteer advertiser for someone else!"

"They're out there, all right."

"... Unless you mean negative publicity, like in today's *Daily Lamp*."

"What about *The Daily Lamp*?" Eminent Li sounded surprised.

"Mr. Li! You didn't see?"

The manager pushed a buzzer, and an intern came in.

"Bring me today's *Daily Lamp*!"

The intern brought a copy of *The Daily Lamp*, and Li saw on the back page that some critic had written a scathing review of the latest publication of Culture Books, *Socializing Techniques for Men and Women*.

The manager waited until he had finished reading.

"Mr. Li!" he exclaimed. "This is a complete broadside. It says nothing about the actual content of the book. We must issue a rejoinder. Not only will this negatively impact the sales of *Socializing Techniques for Men and Women*, which was only just published, but it might impact your reputation as our new marketing director."

"The back page editor for *The Daily Lamp* is named Zhang Dusu. I know him well. As editor, he likes nothing better than lambasting people on a daily basis, just to make a name for himself, no doubt. Moreover, Zhang Dusu's eyes aren't all that sharp. He'll publish any submission that curses people without giving the content a second glance. As a result, contributors who know his temperament are always slandering people right and left to swindle royalties from him. Take today's piece attacking *Socializing Techniques for Men and Women*, for example. The editor published it without ever bothering to actually pick up a copy of the book, so he made a fool of himself. Ha ha ha ha!"

"No matter what, I'm going to have someone issue a rejoinder!"

"Not so fast! He and I are old friends. Let me deal with this."

Despite Eminent Li's promise, the next day in *The Daily Lamp*, *Socializing Techniques for Men and Women* was attacked even more viciously. The critics even went so far as to call it an obscene book. The third and fourth days brought more of the same, but a greater and greater volume: on Day Three two pieces appeared and on Day Four as many as five pieces appeared. The articles took up nearly half the print space, as if it were a special issue dedicated to attacking *Socializing Techniques for Men and Women.*

Strange to say, however, the more brutally *Socializing Techniques for Men and Women* was reviled in the paper, the better it sold. In the past three or four days, twenty thousand copies flew off the shelves. The manager giggled to Eminent Li:

"Haven't you run into Zhang Dusu yet? If not, you might as well hold off a few more days. These past few days we've been cursed like all get out, but sales have also smashed all previous records. *Socializing Techniques for Men and Women* seems to have found its market!"

Eminent Li was unfazed by this revelation and kept smiling, leaving the manager perplexed.

"Mr. Manager! Every one of the pieces cursing *Socializing Techniques for Men and Women* from these past few days was penned by yours truly."

"*You* wrote them? *You* called *Socializing Techniques for Men and Women* an 'obscene book'?"

"Yep! I used different styles of handwriting in the manuscripts I sent Mr. Zhang, who never checked their content and published them all."

"You … what's the big idea?" The manager was none too pleased.

"I'm the director of marketing, so naturally I have to do my job to the best of my abilities. *This*, Mr. Manager, is what I call 'free advertising'!"

The manager was dumbstruck.

"That Zhang Dusu is a professional propagandist."

"Did he agree to help you out because the two of you are old friends?"

"No!" Eminent Li replied. "I used pen names. If he knew it was me he'd never have agreed to publish my pieces. He'd have been too suspicious."

At that moment, the operations manager burst in.

"Mr. Manager! We only have six or seven hundred copies of *Socializing Techniques for Men and Women* left—not nearly enough to meet tomorrow's demand. What should we do? It would take three days to get it reprinted and bound."

"Got it." The manager hastily reached for the phone to call the printers.

The following day, the back page of *The Daily Lamp* said not one word about *Socializing Techniques for Men and Women.* Culture Books' business was of course affected.

The manager summoned Eminent Li for an explanation.

Eminent Li scratched his head.

"This is my fault. I made a mistake yesterday when I was mailing my manuscript to Zhang Dusu: in a moment of forgetfulness I used an envelope with Culture Books' name on it. The game's up! It only occurred to me when I saw that my essay hadn't appeared in the paper. It's over!"

"What a shame! What a shame!"

"Fortunately, the reprints won't be here today anyway, so there's no need to advertise. Once the new books are bound we'll use a new marketing strategy, since the old one has pretty much run its course."

One day about a week later, Manager Zhu of *The Daily Lamp* summoned Zhang Dusu to his office.

"Yesterday at a corporate banquet I sat next to Eminent Li, the marketing director for Culture Books. At the table, in front of everyone, he told me that Zhang Dusu of *The Daily Lamp* never failed to give their books good press because he had received a two hundred dollar stipend from Culture Books. Mr. Zhang! Is this true?"

"God in Heaven! I'm a religious man, and I vow that nothing of the sort has ever happened."

"In that case, why have you exclusively been publishing things about Culture Books for so many days on end, and so many pieces each day? It seems to me that it couldn't be a coincidence."

"I've figured it out now. They sent those manuscripts themselves."

"They mailed you marketing materials and you published each and every one of them? Why, you haven't got a leg to stand on!"

Manager Zhu's expression darkened.

"They tricked me. That Eminent Li who works as their marketing director must be that nasty character Li Ah Mao. The words *Gong Ding* obviously stand in for the character Mao.[4] I gave them free advertising, and he still wrongs me—how infuriating! Li Ah Mao and I are old buddies; how could he make a fool of me like this?"

"And here you've been going around bragging about your 'fifteen years of writing experience'? With so much writing experience, how could you completely lack editorial experience?"

Zhang Dusu was so embarrassed that he wanted to hide his face, and his eyes brimmed with tears.

* * *

4. This rather abstruse joke name alludes to Lord Mao's Pot (Maogongding 毛公鼎), a famous bronze cooking vessel from the Zhou dynasty (1045 BC–AD 256). The pot is inscribed with five hundred characters—more than any other bronze vessel unearthed from that period—and is now considered a national treasure.

## D. HAN EMPEROR GAOZU'S WASHBASIN

One day, a thief named Xiao Wu who worked the train station saw a fifty-something-year-old man place his leather briefcase on the ground as he bought a ticket. Deftly, Xiao Wu snatched the briefcase.

Once he got it home and opened it up to take a look, he discovered it contained only two things: a carved wooden figurine and a letter. The wooden carving was of a woman, but she didn't resemble either the Bodhisattva Guanyin or the Immortal Maiden He.[5] Xiao Wu had no clue what the object was. He concluded that it was just a piece of rotten wood—not worth a dime. *Looks like Xiao Wu's out of luck this time*, he thought. *That old leather briefcase, however, might be worth a couple bucks.*

Xiao Wu then took a look at the letter, which was addressed to "Mr. Wu Jiangcun." He opened it and read the following:

> *My dear Mr. Jiangcun: I have long known you by reputation but regret that we have not yet had the chance to meet. We have made a careful inspection of the antique delivered by Mr. Ye Yufeng and discovered that it dates to the Qin or Han dynasty and is worth a fortune. It is a genuine treasure. Please come and retrieve it at your convenience.*
>
> *At your service,*
> *Wang Fangzhou*
> *Director, Antiquities Research Institute*

As he finished reading the letter, a smile spread across Xiao Wu's face. He took another look at the envelope; the Antiquities

5. Guanyin (full Chinese name: Guanshiyin, from the Sanskrit Avalokiteśvara), the Bodhisattva of Compassion, is one of the most revered deities of the Chinese Buddhist pantheon. Immortal Maiden He, a paragon of purity and wisdom, is the only female member of the Eight Immortals of Chinese Daoist mythology.

Research Institute was at Number 13, Danyang Road. He thought to himself: *Wang Fangzhou has never met Jiangcun before. Why not impersonate the man and go pick up this precious antique myself? Wu Jiangcun must be the man who lost his briefcase at the train station. I could make myself look fifty-something and pay this Wang Fangzhou a visit. The real Wu Jiangcun is fortunately already on the train and unlikely to come back right away. Why don't I just bring this old briefcase with me?* As the thought crossed his mind, he burst out laughing.

He then picked up the wooden carving and said to himself: *This must also be an antique. How could I think it was worthless! I'd better have Wang Fangzhou appraise it too.*

The next morning, Xiao Wu dressed up as a middle-aged gentleman and, with briefcase in hand, went looking for Number 13, Danyang Road, to pay a call on Mr. Wang Fangzhou of the Antiquities Research Institute. An attendant saw him into the reception room and offered him a seat. A short while later, Director Wang Fangzhou, a white-haired old man, hobbled in. Xiao Wu introduced himself as Wu Jiangcun.

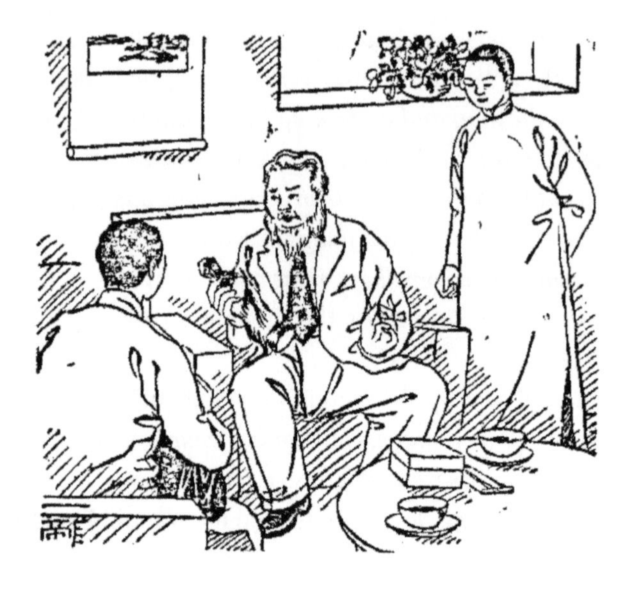

Wang Fangzhou took him at his word and urged him to be seated. Xiao Wu was worried that Wang wouldn't hand over the antique, so he opened the briefcase and produced the letter. Wang immediately responded:

"Mr. Wu! That antique of yours is truly remarkable. Our research has determined that it is a washbasin that belonged to Emperor Gaozu of the Han dynasty. Its total value exceeds fifteen thousand dollars."

Xiao Wu was delighted to hear this but was worried that Wang would become suspicious if he immediately asked for its return.

"Mr. Wu, do you plan to take it home today?"

Xiao Wu jumped at the chance. "Yes."

"Bring out Box #715!"

The attendant left, and Wang Fangzhou smiled: "Mr. Wu, did you bring the receipt?"

Xiao Wu couldn't help but panic at this, but he was a man who knew how to think on his feet.

"Oh, yes. I forgot to bring the receipt when I left home this morning. How about this: I have another antique that I was hoping you could appraise for me while I'm here."

Xiao Wu pulled the wooden carving from the briefcase and handed it to Wang, who seemed delighted to receive it.

"Certainly! It's not a problem that you don't have the receipt. You might as well take the washbasin home with you."

"You can give me a receipt for the wooden carving next time when I bring the receipt for the washbasin."

Xiao Wu thought to himself: the wooden carving is an antique, but it couldn't be worth as much as fifteen thousand dollars, could it?

"Fine."

Just then the attendant brought in an elegant box and set it in front of Xiao Wu.

"It's all yours!" Wang Fangzhou said.

Xiao Wu was eager to see what this precious object looked like, but he was afraid that if he opened the box to take a look he'd give himself away.

Unexpectedly, just at that moment another customer came in, and Xiao Wu was shocked to see that it was none other than the man who lost his briefcase at the station.

"Sorry to trouble you!" the customer said as he came in.

Xiao Wu had no idea what was going on and hurriedly took his leave of Wang Fangzhou, taking the box with him.

Wang Fanzhou handed the wooden carving to Wu Jiangcun. "I've recovered your property for you."

"Sorry to put you through the trouble! This Tang dynasty carving is worth a fortune. Thank you so much, Mr. Li!"

Wang Fangzhou removed his wig and false beard, revealing himself to be Li Ah Mao.

"Come in and have a seat, Mr. Wu! Mr. Wang Fangzhou has something to discuss with you."

Once Xiao Wu was outside he found a quiet spot and opened up the box. But how bizarre! Inside was an earthenware tub which didn't look like anything valuable. Looking closer, he noticed a note on the bottom:

> *This isn't really the Han emperor Gaozu's washbasin; it's my dog's food dish. You'll find it useful in the future when you go begging. A special present for you.*
>
> *Li Ah Mao*

* * *

**E. DATE PITS WITH HOLES**

"Your rent's going up no matter what," Old Xiao, the subletting landlord, told Li Ah Mao with a stern expression.

"Think about it!" Mrs. Xiao chimed in. "Nowadays the price of everything has gone up ten-fold. You'll be getting a real bargain renting my room even for *sixty* dollars a month. Did you really think you'd be able to rent it for just *six*?"

Li Ah Mao lowered his head and was silent for a moment. This couple wouldn't budge an inch. Then he spoke up: "What'll you do if I don't pay more?"

"We'd have to ask you to move out!" Old Xiao replied.

"So be it. I'll be out by the end of the month."

Just as he finished speaking, Ah Mao glanced at the floor and a look of surprise crossed his face. He quickly kneeled down and picked up a tiny object.

"Where did this come from?"

The couple looked in his hand and saw that it was a date pit. Just now, Mrs. Xiao had eaten a date and spit the pit onto the floor.

"What about it?" Mrs. Xiao couldn't help feeling puzzled.

"Where did this come from? Will you sell it to me? How much do you want for it?"

Seeing Ah Mao so deliriously happy, Old Xiao piped up too: "What's this all about?"

"You have to let me buy it!"

As he spoke, Ah Mao pulled out his wallet, placed the date pit inside, and produced a one-dollar bill, which he handed to Mrs. Xiao.

"Thank you!"

Today's rampant inflation notwithstanding, Mrs. Xiao was skeptical that a date pit on the floor could fetch one dollar.

"It's yours, but what good is it to you? You've got to tell us what's going on."

"Mrs. Xiao!" Ah Mao chuckled as he put away his wallet, "A merchant from Jiangxi Province has recently been buying these up."

"Really? Are date pits some kind of treasure?"

"No! This one is unique. See? It has two holes on the top. The traveler is buying all two-holed date pits he can get a hold of. It's supposedly for making medicine. In the three or four months he's been here, he's already bought quite a few."

"Are you sure that the pit you just bought had two holes in the top?" Old Xiao asked.

"Of course! Would I have paid a dollar for something that belongs in the rubbish bin?"

"Mr. Li, take it out again and let us have a look."

Ah Mao shook his head.

"For crying out loud!" Mrs. Li exclaimed. "Are you afraid we'll steal it back and refuse to sell it to you? Fine. So, how much will you be able to sell it to that traveler for?"

Ah Mao smiled but kept silent.

"If I buy another ten catties of dates to eat tomorrow, I should be able to find a bunch of pits with holes, right?" Mrs. Xiao asked hopefully.

"Nope! I've heard that it's hard to find a single one in a thousand. You might not even find one in ten or twenty catties. You might as well trying buying one or two piculs!"[6]

Mrs. Xiao colored.

"You can make medicine from it? What does it cure?"

"It's a secret. I couldn't tell you."

With that, Ah Mao went upstairs.

One afternoon a week or so later, there was a knock at the door. Old Xiao was bedridden with his old malady, scrotal eczema, so Mrs. Xiao answered the door.

"Is Mr. Li home?" asked the youth at the door.

"Not now. He went out this morning."

"What rotten timing! And I came such a long way. What do I do now?"

6. One catty is approximately 600 grams; one picul is a little over sixty kilos.

"Is there a problem?"

"You bet there is! He specially asked me to deliver the date pits I collected in the countryside today." So saying, he lifted the small bag he was carrying.

"Date pits with holes?" Mrs. Xiao asked delightedly. "How many did you collect?"

"After two months of searching, I was only able to collect a hundred."

"A hundred! That's quite a feat!" Thinking for a moment, she asked: "How much were you planning to sell them to Mr. Li for, then?"

"Fifty cents each!"

"Fifty cents each would be fifty dollars for the hundred. How about this: since we don't know when Mr. Li will be home, why don't you give them to me and I'll give you the fifty dollars?"

"That'd be great!"

With that, he opened the little bag and, sure enough, it was filled with date pits. Mrs. Li picked one up and saw that it indeed had two small holes.

Mrs. Li thought to herself: *When Ah Mao gets back I can sell them to him for a dollar each and clear fifty dollars on the deal.*

She paid, got the goods, and the young man left. Examining the pits closely, she saw that each had two holes. They were the genuine article all right.

Li Ah Mao returned after the Xiaos had finished dinner, but Mrs. Xiao didn't mention the events of the day. She went upstairs and saw when she reached Ah Mao's room that he was in the middle of reading a book entitled *How to Promote Longevity.*

"Mr. Li!"

Ah Mao looked back and saw Mrs. Li holding a small bag.

"Today I had someone find a bunch of date pits with holes, one hundred all together. I'll sell them to you at the usual price: one dollar each!"

So saying, she opened the bag.

Ah Mao balked. "Aiya! That Jiangxi merchant left town yesterday!"

Mr. Xiao was taken aback but immediately regained her composure. "That's all right. You can take them now and sell them to him the next time he comes by."

"I'm not going to shell out a hundred dollars not knowing when he'll be back! Besides, right now I need to prepare my moving expenses. The price of renting a moving truck has gone up again—it now costs twenty dollars per hour!"

"How about if I lower the price a bit, then?" Mrs. Xiao asked, anxiously.

"I don't have any use for them now that the buyer is gone. What would I do with them?"

"What illness do these cure, after all? You must know! Why won't you tell me?"

Ah Mao just smiled and there was nothing the landlord's wife could do about it, so she left.

The next day, while Ah Mao was out, Mrs. Xiao snuck into his room and took a peek at *How to Promote Longevity*, hoping to discover the secret. Sure enough, she found a note stuck between the pages:

"Date pits with two holes on the top, pan fried and fed to the patient as a soup, can cure inflammation of the scrotum."

Mrs. Xiao was beside herself with delight and hurried back downstairs to tell Old Xiao: "Good news: I've got a cure."

By the time Mrs. Xiao had fried up the date pits for Old Xiao to eat, Li Ah Mao had just moved out and his friend, Big Brother Xue, stopped by to pay him a visit.

"I'm going to treat you to dinner today!" Ah Mao told him.

"What's got you feeling so rich?"

"I've still got a bunch of cash left over after paying for the moving truck out of the fifty dollars I got from the landlady, so I ought to treat you."

"That's right. I spent two hours burning little holes in date pits with a pipe pick."

"I also pan-fried the pits in croton oil. When Old Xiao eats them today, he's sure to get diarrhea."

The two men looked at each other and smiled.

* * *

## F. THE PEARL NECKLACE

In this morning's newspaper, a headline about a shocking robbery jumped out at the reader in bold type:

### ROBBERY AT NO. 39, TAIPING ROAD

*Last night a banquet was held at the residence of the rich gentleman Roll N. Doh at No. 39, Taiping Road. The party was attended by thirty or forty guests, all distinguished personages. Just as the party was wrapping up, the lights suddenly went out, momentarily plunging the entire house into darkness and chaos. Someone was dispatched to procure candles while the switchbox was repaired. In the darkness, a pearl necklace worth thirty thousand dollars was snatched from the neck of Madame Doh. By the time the police arrived, the lights had been repaired and the room was again illuminated. Given the suspicious circumstances, the police questioned every guest before allowing them to leave. The investigation concluded that an artist named Flowery Huang was the most likely suspect, as he and Mr. Doh had been acquainted for less than a week. That evening, the banquet had been set to begin at 7:00, but Flowery Huang arrived at the Doh residence at 6:00. At that time, Mr. and Madame Doh were still out and Flowery Huang was alone in the guest reception room for an hour. The police frisked Flowery Huang but were unable to find the necklace, or even a single handkerchief in his pocket. Lacking any evidence, the police were compelled to release him, and the case is at present completely murky.*

As Lao Ping finished reading this news item aloud to his friend Li Ah Mao, he eagerly asked Li: "Can you figure this one out?"

"What's to figure out? The matter's as simple as can be!"

"In that case, who stole the pearl necklace?"

"That artist Flowery Huang, of course. That goes without saying."

Lao Ping was stunned. "But didn't they say that they couldn't find even a handkerchief on him?"

"That's right. It's precisely *because* they couldn't find a handkerchief on him that we know he's the one who stole the pearl necklace."

"But why?"

"Think about it: every middle- and upper-class man, without exception, sports a handkerchief. For an artist like him who has social relations with rich and high-status families to go without a handkerchief would be a capital crime. This is the detail with which we can crack the case."

Lao Ping mulled this over aloud:

"I can see how the detectives might be able to crack the case if they found *something* on the suspect, but how could they crack it if they found *nothing* on him?"

Ah Mao smiled.

"Flowery Huang had a handkerchief to begin with, and then he used it to wrap up the pearl necklace in a parcel. That's why the handkerchief wasn't on his person. If it were me, I'd have had two handkerchiefs ready: one for wrapping up the necklace, and one to keep on me. An ironclad plan like that would have made this an impossible case to crack."

Hearing this, Lao Ping cheered up. "Since you know how the thief stole the necklace, you could be of immense help to the police in their investigations. Where is the pearl necklace now? Once they've found the evidence, Flowery Huang will be cornered for sure."

Ah Mao shook his head. "It's too late for that. By now Flowery Huang's accomplice will have long since hidden the necklace in some safe place. If, within half an hour of last night's incident, someone had figured out their scheme and nabbed them immediately, they'd have had the culprits and the evidence in hand. There's nothing to be done now."

Ah Mao glanced at Lao Ping. "You probably still haven't quite got it figured out, have you? Let me explain it to you once again in detail. At six o'clock last night Flowery Huang arrived at the Doh residence and had one hour to himself. During this time, he did two things: first, he stole a light bulb from the many lamps in the Doh household. No one would notice something like that. Second, he brought with him a ball of string. On the north side of the reception room he tied one end of the string to the steel hook that fastens the window in place on the outside of the windowsill. He then threw the ball of string out the window. He must have arranged for an accomplice to be waiting outside. By that time the sky was already dark, so no one would have been able to see the string. As the banquet was breaking up, he stuck something—anything would do—into the empty light bulb socket to cause a short-circuit. As soon as the lights went out, he snatched Madame Doh's pearl necklace, wrapped it up in his handkerchief, and attached it to the string outside the window, along which it naturally slid into the hands of his accomplice. A few seconds later, Flowery Huang untied the string for his accomplice to take with him, leaving no trace. In the next ten minutes the accomplice would of course have spirited the pearl necklace off to a safe place. Do you get it now, Lao Ping?"

Lao Ping chuckled. "I get it! That said, it's more than a bit suspicious that someone who wasn't on the scene would be able to describe what happened so vividly!"

Li Ah Mao responded with a knowing smile. "So you suspect me of being Flowery Huang, do you? Or perhaps the accomplice in the empty room? Ha ha!"

* * *

## G. THE OVERNIGHT FORTUNETELLER

People crowded around the glyphomancy stall.[7] Brother Ah Mao and Brother Ah Ping went over to take a look and saw that the onlookers were all peasants from the countryside. Two words graced a small, wooden placard on the table: "Overnight fortune-telling." The fortuneteller, sporting a worn-out hat, called out:

"I can foretell whether your parents are alive or not and how many brothers you have."

Just then, a man came forward to have his fortune told.

"Are both your parents living?"

"They're both dead."

"How many brothers do you have?"

---

7. Glyphomancy (*chai zi* 拆字) is a traditional Chinese fortunetelling practice in which the characters in a person's name are disaggregated into component parts and compared with their horoscope or other personal particulars to determine their circumstances or prognosticate their future.

"Two!"

The fortuneteller pulled out an envelope and unfolded it to reveal nine words written on a letter inside:

"NO MOTHER FATHER LIVING BROTHERS THREE KINGDOMS ONE BRANCH"

The fortuneteller chuckled:

"As you can see, I foretold this long ago."

With that, he took up a red brush and punctuated the line as follows:

"NO MOTHER FATHER LIVING. BROTHERS: THREE KINGDOMS – ONE BRANCH"

Putting down his brush, he said:

"Your father and mother are gone, and you have two brothers. Subtract one from the three brothers of the *Three Kingdoms* and you're left with two.[8] Works, doesn't it? I foretold your circumstances last night."

So saying, he handed him the letter and envelope.

"If you yourself can't read, you can go ask someone who can."

One fortune told, another customer stepped up.

"Are both of your parents living?"

"My father is, but my mother is gone."

"How many brothers do you have?"

"Four."

"Good. I knew it."

Again he pulled out an envelope, opened it to reveal the same

---

8. *Three Kingdoms* is an epic Ming dynasty (1368–1644) novel about the fall of the Han dynasty and its partition intro three warring kingdoms. The "three brothers" referred to here are Liu Bei, a royal kinsman of the Han; Guan Yu, a fugitive; and a butcher, Zhang Fei. Originally strangers, the unlikely trio recognize each others' virtue and swear an oath of brotherhood in a peach orchard, the peach being a symbol of loyalty. For a description of the brotherhood's role in the story, see Moss Roberts's afterword to his translation of the novel, *Three Kingdoms* (University of California Press, 1991), pp. 944–945.

nine words, and again used his red brush to punctuate the line as follows:

"NO MOTHER. FATHER LIVING. BROTHERS: THREE KINGDOMS + ONE BRANCH"

He handed the paper to the man:

"You're illiterate? Let me explain what it says: Your mother is dead, your father is alive, and you have four brothers. Doesn't three brothers plus one equal four? No mistake."

The second fortune told, a third person came forward.

"Are both of your parents living?"

"Yes."

"How many brothers do you have?"

"Just one."

"Good. Take a look."

He pulled out a third envelope, opened it to reveal the same nine words, and marked the words in red as follows:

"~~NO~~ MOTHER, FATHER LIVING. BROTHERS: THREE KINGDOMS = ONE BRANCH"

He put down his brush.

"Your father is alive, as is your mother, and you have only one brother—like a single branch broken off in the peach orchard of the *Three Kingdoms*."

By that time, the peasant onlookers, though they didn't understand what he was writing, were all convinced that his fortunetelling really worked. People who had had their fortunes told held onto their piece of paper reverently, and went home to show to someone who knew how to read.

Having witnessed all this, Brother Ah Mao and Brother Ah Ping also left.

"Even though he's duping all those illiterate people, you've got to hand it to him that he came up with a great all-purpose line." Ah Mao remarked.

"I saw a different overnight fortuneteller at the city god temple. Now *his* technique was truly efficacious. He could tell someone's name, age, and home address—that was *real* overnight fortunetelling."

"I don't believe it. When it comes down to it, all these drifters are frauds."

"Not at all! I'll take you there. I guarantee you'll be impressed when you see him in action."

"All right, let's go."

The two of them walked over to the boulevard where the city god temple was located and saw a fortuneteller sitting in a tiny room, facing westward. The room was divided in two by a wooden partition: the front was the fortunetelling space and the back was probably a bedroom. The left side of the fortunetelling table was flush against the wall. By this time, quite a crowd of onlookers had gathered, and the fortuneteller was questioning a young man.

"Your honorable name, sir?"

"My humble surname is Fang and my name Danian. 'Da' as in 'great' and 'nian' as in 'year.'"

"Your present age? What was the month, day, and time of your birth?"

"I am thirty-eight and was born between 11 p.m. and 1 a.m. on July 15th."

"Are your parents both living?"

"My father is dead; my mother's living."

"How many brothers?"

"Five."

"Marital status?"

"My first wife died and I've remarried."

"Children?"

"Two daughters."

"Home address?"

"Number 3, Taiping Bridge."

Having finished his questioning, the fortuneteller addressed the crowd:

"Ladies and gentlemen! You've all heard this gentleman's words. Please mark them well."

With that, he opened a drawer, reached inside, and produced an envelope. He tore open the envelope, tossed it into a wastepaper basket, and then unfolded the letter. On it, everyone read the following:

Name: Fang Danian
Age: 38. Born between 11 p.m. and 1 a.m. on July 15th
Parents: Father dead, mother living
Brothers: Five
Marital status: Remarried
Children: Two daughters
Address: Number 3, Taiping Bridge

Below this was a long paragraph of prognostications about fortune and misfortune, the accuracy of which it was too soon to verify. The particulars written above, however, set the onlookers' a-titter.

"What do you think?" Brother Ah Ping asked Brother Ah Mao.

Brother Ah Mao didn't respond and looked around as if he were more interested in the layout of the room than in the fortuneteller himself.

"What do you think if I go have my fortune told too?" Brother Ah Ping asked, seeing Brother Ah Mao's unresponsiveness. Brother Ah Mao smiled at him, as if to signal that he didn't object.

"Sir!" Brother Ah Mao suddenly addressed the fortuneteller.

"You'd like your fortune told?" came the reply.

"No! Is there a place around here to go pee?"

The crowd laughed.

"Yes. Go to the small courtyard out back."

Brother Ah Mao nodded and went into the courtyard to relieve himself. Brother Ah Ping, of course, stepped up to have his fortune told.

"Your honorable name, sir?"

"My name is Bai Ping: 'Bai' as in 'white' and 'Ping' as in 'duck-weed.'"

"Your current age and when were you born?"

"I'm twenty-nine and was born between 7:00 and 9:00 a.m. on March 28th."

"Are both your parents living?"

"My father's alive, and my 'mother' is my stepmother."

"How many brothers?"

"Three."

"Marital status?"

"Married."

"Children?"

"One son and one daughter."

"Home address?"

"Number 90, Longmen Road."

Having finished his questioning, the fortuneteller repeated his usual spiel:

"Ladies and gentlemen! Keep this gentleman's words in mind. I wrote them down long ago."

So saying, he opened the left drawer and took out another envelope. As before, he tore open the envelope and spread out the letter, on which everyone read the following:

Name: Bai Ping
Age: 9. Born on June 6th between 7:00 and 9:00 p.m.
Parents: Three fathers, one mother
Brothers: Younger brother died south of the Yangtze, elder brother died in the Mongolian north
Marital status: Sold wife to a bachelor
Children: One son and one daughter, both fathered by another man
Address: King of Hell Road, on the Bridge of No Return

Everyone burst out laughing. Brother Ah Ping was so furious that all the blood rushed to his face, and he collared the fortuneteller and gave him a slap across the face. The fortuneteller, meanwhile, was dumbfounded by what he saw on that piece of paper and, after being slapped, turned around and tried to escape into the bedroom.

To his surprise, he bumped into Brother Ah Mao who just that moment was coming out. Li Ah Mao chuckled:

"Sir! Your assistant requested leave, so I stepped in for him. Ha ha ha ha!"

Brother Ah Ping and the rest of the audience went into the inner room where they saw a man tied to a chair with a wad of cotton stuffed in his mouth, secured by a handkerchief tied around his head. In front was a desk, at which he used to sit and fill in the data from overheard questions and answers. Everyone also saw a hole in the wall, which led into the desk drawer on the other side.

Realizing they'd been had, the crowd dispersed, not bothering to settle accounts with this itinerant swindler.

After Brother Ah Mao and Brother Ah Ping stepped back outside, Brother Ah Mao produced a letter, which he showed to Ah Ping by way of explanation:

"This letter is quite clever too: there's a fold on the back which is like a door curtain. The paper inside is folded just right so that he could fill in the name, age, parents, and other items without having to open the envelope and reseal it. That's why when the fortuneteller brought it out of the envelope he couldn't just unseal it but instead had to tear it open to avoid revealing the ploy. Not bad, wouldn't you say?"

Brother Ah Ping was still annoyed.

"Some practical joke! How could you say I had three fathers and married off my wife to a bachelor, you darn scoundrel!"

* * *

## H. PLEASE EXIT THROUGH THE BACK DOOR

At a time when unemployed people were being churned out at a rapid rate, a pair of friends, newly jobless, appeared on Li Ah Mao's doorstep. One was named Brother Ah Yang, the other Brother Ah Ping.

Brother Ah Yang was a garden designer by profession. Recently, however, everyone was too busy trying to buy rice to think about designing gardens. Brother Ah Yang consequently had shut down his garden supply store, and he was out of a job.

Brother Ah Ping owned a barber shop, which had once done a brisk business. Recently, however, the price of scissors, razors, shampoo, and the like had spiraled out of control, and with rice now costing so much he was having real trouble providing for his employees. He could, of course, raise prices, but the moment customers saw that the price of a haircut had gone up they would all start putting off their next trim. A customer who came in once every twenty days would now come in only every thirty days, and one who came in every thirty days wouldn't come in more than once every month and a half. Faced with this situation, Brother Ah Ping was ready to close up shop too.

Today, both were calling on Brother Ah Mao to ask for his suggestions on how they might get back on their feet.

Brother Ah Yang asked Brother Ah Mao to suggest what type of business he should get into now that his shop was closed.

Brother Ah Ping hadn't closed his shop yet, but he'd already decided to do so and was also seeking Brother Ah Mao's help in finding a new livelihood.

"If I continue to stay unemployed like this it's going to be a serious problem," Brother Ah Yang said. "Brother Ah Mao! You're a supreme slacker of the modern age. You must have some new get-rich scheme to teach us."

"You're not doing so bad, Brother Ah Yang!" Brother Ah Ping interjected.

"What do you mean 'not so bad'?—I'm unemployed!"

"Could be worse! You're out of a job, but you can get by with just living expenses. For me it's more serious: besides having to scrape together living expenses, I'm losing money every day my shop stays open. I'm losing more money than you, so I need Brother Ah Mao's help even more critically."

Brother Ah Mao listened to the two of them, thought for a moment, and then said, "If you're already unemployed, clearly the thing to do is to forge a new path. If you aren't yet out of a job, however, you should keep your current one going."

Brother Ah Ping shook his head.

"I can't keep bleeding money like this."

Brother Ah Mao took a drag on his cigarette and exhaled a puff of smoke. "The two of you live at the same place, right?"

"That's right!" Brother Ah Yang said. "I live at No. 174 Danyang

Road and sell garden supplies out the front door. His barber shop, at No. 71, Zhenjiang Road, shares a back door with mine."

"Excellent!" Brother Ah Mao smiled. "I've come up with a brilliant scheme for the two of you. Brother Ah Yang's given up his old profession, so he'll change to a new one, and Brother Ah Ping will continue in his current trade. I guarantee the two of you will strike it rich."

Three days later, two unusual advertisements suddenly appeared in the newspaper:

**Fast-Acting Miracle Hair Tonic for the Bald**

| | |
|---|---|
| Tested on the premises | Incomparably efficacious |
| Five dollars per packet | Instructions enclosed |

No. 174, Danyang Road
Brother Ah Yang, Inventor

**New, Super-Economical Head-Shaving Method**

| | |
|---|---|
| A clean shave in one go | Costs only a dime |
| The secret revealed | Taught to one and all |
| A complete course of instruction | Fee: three dollars |

Quick Blade Barber Shop, No. 71, Zhenjiang Road
Brother Ah Ping, Proprietor

After these two advertisements appeared, Brother Ah Yang and Brother Ah Ping's shop fronts were as busy as all get out. Above each doorway hung a white cotton cloth banner with enormous characters on it, which served as a temporary shop sign.

Strange to say! Passersby on the street could all see for themselves that the men going in Brother Ah Yang's door were all bald. Clearly, they were there to buy hair tonic. Soon afterward, the men could be seen reemerging one by one, each with a thick head of hair and holding in his hand a paper packet, which was of course the so-called miracle tonic. Remarkably enough, not a single bald man could be found among the customers coming out of the shop! The news passed by word of mouth from one person to ten and from ten to a hundred until everyone had urged their bald friends and family members to go buy this miracle tonic.

Across the street from Quick Blade Barber Shop at No. 71, Zhenjiang Road, there happened to be a teahouse. Today, patrons on both floors saw a cloth banner above the door to the barbershop with the words: *New, super-economical head-shaving method.* As they watched, groups of men with wild and unkempt hair went in one after another, and, a moment later, each emerged clean-shaven. Naturally, this astounding miracle startled everyone. Word spread widely, and everyone went to find out what this new, super-economical head-shaving method was all about.

And just like that, Brother Ah Yang and Brother Ah Ping were rolling in dough. Both were immensely grateful to Li Ah Mao.

In fact, the trick, once revealed, is not worth a laugh. When bald men entered Brother Ah Yang's door to buy tonic they saw a paper note pasted next to the cabinet, which read:

*Due to the large number of customers,*
*please exit through the back door.*

Accordingly, each bald customer exited through Brother Ah Ping's barber shop. The men looking for a new, super-economical head-shaving method, meanwhile, stepped inside Quick Blade Barber Shop and paid their three dollars for a tightly-sealed bag, on which was written: *To be opened at home.* On the wall they saw a sign:

*Due to the large number of customers,*
*please exit through the back door.*

Accordingly, they all exited through Brother Ah Yang's front door, and everyone who saw the bag in their hand thought it was the miracle hair tonic!

In fact, the course of instruction for this so-called new, super-economical head-shaving method, despite its three-dollar price tag, consisted of only a few lines, which can be shared with the reader:

*Before bed, mix a centigram of flour into a paste and rub into your hair, and then go to bed. In the middle of the night, rats will come to eat the paste, and in the process chew your hair down to the nub.*

As for Brother Ah Yang's miracle hair tonic, it was nothing but a bag of fertilizer. The instructions contained a few cheeky lines, which read as follows:

*Grass will grow if this powder is applied to soil, but not to stone. Should you find that this tonic doesn't work on your head, it means your honorable noggin must be made of rock. In that case, drill a few small holes in your skull and reapply as a paste. If that doesn't work, transplanting fine rattan fibers into your scalp might look pretty too.*

* * *

## I. MOVING PERMIT

Brother Ah Mao hurried over to Brother Ah Yang's house only to find the latter sitting there looking down in the dumps.

"What's wrong? Why did you send someone to tell me to rush over?"

Brother Ah Yang replied: "I can't believe it. Someone's been killed."

With that, Brother Ah Yang stood up and hastily pulled Brother Ah Mao inside.

Brother Ah Mao entered the room with him and saw lying on the bed the corpse of a man he'd never seen before.

"Who's this?"

"His name's Kit D. Bouquet. He and I had something of a grudge against each other. Last night in the middle of the night he came over and insisted on spending the night here. Little did I know that he had taken poison before coming over, and that before dawn the poison would take effect and kill him. Sounds like he had it in for me, doesn't it?"

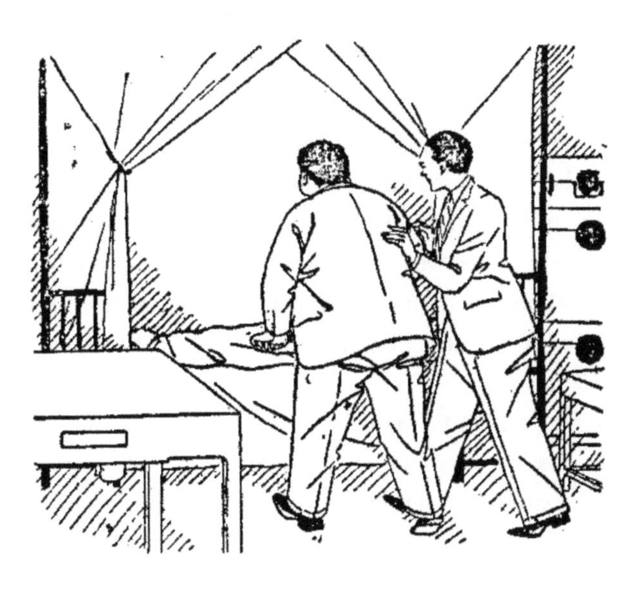

"Did he really come over just for revenge?"

"What else could it be?"

"What did he expect to gain by sacrificing his own life?" Brother Ah Mao wondered, puzzled.

"Maybe his family members will come to extort money from me!"

Brother Ah Yang began to panic.

"Do his family members know he died here?"

"I don't know!"

"What do you plan to do now?"

"I asked you to come here and talk it over because I couldn't think of anything."

Brother Ah Mao thought for a while and then spoke:

"Does he have a family?"

"I don't know!"

"The way I see it, it's possible that he doesn't. Or, even if he does, it's possible that they don't know about what happened."

"Why?"

"Otherwise, why hasn't anyone come by now that he's dead?"

"It doesn't sound like such a big problem, the way you put it. But even if no one's come to extort money, how am I supposed to deal with this corpse?"

Brother Ah Mao smiled. "That's easy. I'll help you deal with it. That said, we can't be sure that the family of the dead man won't come by, so the first thing you need to do right away is move house. Fortunately, you don't have a family or much furniture, so you can take your stuff out the back door today, and if you don't have a place to store it you can move it over to my place. I've got it all covered."

"I won't be able to find a new place just like that, so I'll move to your place for the time being. Thanks for everything you're doing for me."

"Great! Let's set to work!"

Now that they had a plan, Brother Ah Yang was finally able to cast off the stone that had been weighing down his heart.

* * *

An hour later, the strip of paper with the words "Yang Residence" that had been pasted over Brother Ah Yang's door disappeared and was replaced with one that read "Number One Silver Co."

At the same time, passersby saw trunk after trunk of money being carried in.

This was Brother Ah Mao's little game.

In fact, there was only one trunk. It was indeed the type that banks use for storing cash, but no one knew what was really inside. Ah Mao hired two temporary workers to carry it in the front door, and then out the back door and back around to the front door, so that it looked like many trunks to onlookers when in fact there was just one. Soon, all of Brother Ah Mao's furniture was moved out.

One of the people on the street who watched what was going on was none other than the thief Bachelor Wang. Seeing trunk after trunk of money being carried into this silver company, Bachelor Wang couldn't help turning green with envy.

* * *

That evening, Bachelor Wang arranged for two of his comrades to meet him at midnight by the back door of Brother Ah Yang's house and help dig a hole under the wall. Bachelor Wang took the lead himself, digging the hole and wriggling his way inside. Suddenly, his heart began thumping wildly. Calmly pulling down his pants, he took a poop on the floor. Once finished, he felt more relaxed and his heartrate returned to normal. Meanwhile, one of his partners kept watch while the other came in to help.

Looking around, Bachelor Wang saw that the room was empty: no furniture, no trunks filled with cash. Only one trunk was there, but it was empty. Besides this, there was only a long wooden box nailed tightly shut, which contained who knows what.

Bachelor Wang thought to himself: "This is obviously where they stored the cash from all those trunks I saw today."

Bachelor Wang couldn't wait to open it, so, throwing caution to the wind, the three accomplices went to fetch a rope and a crowbar, forced open the back door, and lugged the wooden box home.

The journey home went without a hitch, and the three were beside themselves with joy.

Back home, the three of them rushed to open the top and received a shock when they looked inside: it wasn't cash, it was a corpse!

"Ah! It's a person!"

"He's kicked the bucket!"

That's right: it was Kit D. Bouquet's corpse. Had Kit D. Bouquet heard them, his ghost would undoubtedly have been shocked that these three strangers knew his name.

The three of them searched the body.

"Crud! There's not a single buck on this guy!"

"What good's a corpse?"

Taking a closer look, Bachelor Wang saw that the corpse appeared to hold a note in its right hand. Bachelor Wang reached out to take it from him, and the three men read together:

**Moving Permit**

Product name: Fresh dead man
Quantity: 1
Weight: 83 pounds
Shipper: Li Ah Mao
Origin: Number One Silver Co., No. 13, Danyang Rd.
Destination: Uncle Thief's house
Moving motive: Wants to get rich
Moving time: Midnight tonight
Moving method: Volunteer labor

Reading this, the three men couldn't help sucking in a breath of cold air!

* * *

## J. THE LOCKOUT

Late at night, Li Ah Mao was upstairs reading a book when he heard his next door neighbor, Brother Ah Yang, sighing and moaning dispiritedly. Brother Ah Mao struck up a conversation with him:

"Brother Ah Yang! What's got you so down in the dumps?"

"Ai! Brother Ah Mao! Don't get me started. It's already the middle of the night and my wife still hasn't come home. It's such a pain to be stuck waiting for her like this! It's not just today either; I go through this every night."

"That's your own fault."

"How could it be *my* fault?"

"A wise man once said: 'Only women and petty-minded men are hard to reform.' If you don't show your wife who's boss and you let her run around like this instead, of course she's going to be out of control."

"Tell me, then! How should I instruct her?"

"Step Number One is the lockout."

"'The lockout'? What's 'the lockout'?"

"When she comes home tonight, keep the door shut no matter what. That's the lockout."

"What do I do after I lock her out?"

"Second, give her a good scolding from the second-story window. Don't let her in until she surrenders and begs for mercy. This'll assure that in the future your honorable wife will come home earlier every day."

* * *

"Open up! Open up!"

"Who is it?"

"Old Yang, it's me! Quick, open up!"

"It's you? What are you doing coming home in the middle of the night?"

"I was playing mahjong at my sister's house."

"You good-for-nothing! You're a married woman, but instead of keeping house you abandon your loving husband and go out to play mahjong. Some lady of the house you are!"

"Old Yang! Have you gone crazy all of a sudden? I play mahjong every night!"

"You had this coming. What kind of disgraceful person plays mahjong every night? From today onward I'm going to have to tighten the screws on you. For the moment, there's nothing more to say. The door's staying shut and that's that."

"Hurry and open up! If you don't, I'll break this door down."

Silence.

"You really aren't going to open it? Old Yang! I've been your wife for seven or eight years now; how could you pull a stunt like this? How could you let your dear wife stand out in the street all night? My darling! Open up, open up!"

Still, silence.

"Are you going to open up or aren't you? Just going to keep it shut your whole life, then? Fine! How could I have married such an uncaring husband? If this is what life is going to be like, I'd rather die."

She picked up a large stone from the road and carried it over to the canal behind their house.

*Ker-splash!*

Hearing this, Brother Ah Yang knew that his wife had jumped into the river. What if she drowned!? Racing downstairs, he opened the door and went outside to see what had happened.

At that moment, his wife snuck inside and quickly locked the door behind her. Brother Ah Yang, not finding anything out of the ordinary, went back to the front door only to find it locked. Starting to fret, he knocked on the door three times.

"Who's knocking?" his wife called from the upstairs window.

"You tricked me! Hurry and open up!"

"It's you, is it? What are you doing coming home in the middle of the night? You're a married man, but instead of keeping house you abandon your loving wife—you must have been out playing mahjong! Some master of the house you are!"

"Fine, fine, we're quits! Open up!"

"What kind of disgraceful person plays mahjong every night? From today onward I'm going to have to tighten the screws on you. For the moment, there's nothing more to say. The door's staying shut and that's that."

Brother Ah Yang didn't know whether to laugh or cry. Looking up at the next door building, he saw Brother Ah Mao looking out the window and appealed to him for backup.

"Brother Ah Mao! You told me to lock her out, but now she's locked *me* out."

"So what?"

"Don't kick me while I'm down. Help me figure something out, quick."

"Relax! I'll get that door open. Why don't you spend the night at my place? When Sister Cassia comes back from the dance hall we can party the night away."

Mrs. Yang heard every word. Was she going to let that happen? Quickly and silently, she cracked open the door and went out to drag Brother Ah Yang back. Little did she expect to find no trace of him, and that when she turned around her own door was shut behind her! Looking up, she saw Brother Ah Yang in the upstairs window laughing heartily:

"Thanks, Ah Mao!"

"Brother Ah Yang, go to bed!"

"So, is Sister Cassia coming or what?"

"No way! Tonight she'll probably be locked out on the road!"

* * *

## K. JAPANESE SCHOOL

"These days have been a real killer! My salary's not so bad—three hundred dollars a month—but it's not enough to buy a picul of rice. Think about it, Brother Ah Mao! How am I supposed to get by? Clothes, food, rent, and transportation all cost money, but my entire salary goes to rice. How am I supposed to cover the rest of it?"

From his second-floor window, Brother Ah Yang was chatting with his next-door neighbor, Brother Ah Mao.

"You should find yourself some sort of new line of business or other!" Brother Ah Mao replied solicitously.

"What kind of business could I do? Everyone's either got a monopoly or is short of stock. What room is left for people like us to do business?"

"Keep thinking. There must be some line of business to get into."

"Ai! Even if we make money, we'll still be up the creek since we'll have to finagle rice, cooking oil, and charcoal briquettes. It's enough to push one over the edge!"

Brother Ah Mao nodded.

"Getting those basic necessities is a challenge alright. We should think of some way to get them without having to go to all that trouble."

Brother Ah Yang seemed excited by this.

"Brother Ah Mao! You sound so calm. Have you already found some new type of employment for us?"

"Yep."

"What is it? Tell me!"

"We could do any kind of business we want. It occurs to me that one could make a killing by opening a Japanese language school."

"You're right, of course, but you and I are in the same boat: we can't speak a word of Japanese."

Brother Ah Mao smiled.

"To tell the truth, I've already decided to open a Japanese school."

"But then you'll have to pay big money to hire someone to teach. What's the point in that?"

"No I won't! I'll do the teaching myself."

"Absurd! What do you know?"

"Don't make fun of me! I read a book called *Japanese in One Day* and am already fluent."

"Ha ha! What a faker!"

"I'll post the ad for enrollments tomorrow. It's a new scheme—no tuition."

"No tuition? What's in it for you, then?"

"Every month, each student has to give me one peck of white rice."

"So, rice in lieu of tuition?"

"That's it!"

"Oh! Ten students would get you one picul, and a hundred students would get you ten piculs. Ha ha! You could start a rice warehouse!"

* * *

"*Ko-me*!"

"*Ko-me*!"

Ah Mao read aloud, and the students recited with him.

"Enunciate: *ko-me*."

"*Ko-me*."

After teaching the Japanese alphabets, Ah Mao taught one word per day. After three weeks, the students were feeling somewhat dissatisfied:

"Teacher! Please continue to the next part of the lesson!"

"*Ko-me*!"

"Teacher! We already know that one. Please teach us some new words."

"No go! Stop your jabbering! Who's teaching who here?" Ah Mao scowled at his students.

"Teacher, what does *kome* mean?"

"*Kome* means 'rice.' Got it?"

The students nodded.

"Teacher, please continue to the next part of the lesson. We've already mastered 'rice.' Don't just endlessly repeat this one word."

"Keep quiet!" Brother Ah Mao looked mad. "Here I'm not even charging you tuition, and you start acting up."

"Teacher, we might not be paying tuition, but we did bring you rice."

"Well, what's wrong with me teaching you how to say 'rice' when you've brought me rice?"

"Please continue to the next part of the lesson anyway. We already understand 'rice.'"

"The new lesson will have to wait until next month."

The students looked at each other.

"On the first of next month, you won't have to bring rice. I've changed the regulations. Instead, each student should bring four liters of cooking oil. Starting the first of next month, we'll begin Lesson Two."

* * *

The following month, all the students really did bring cooking oil in lieu of tuition, and, sure enough, they began a new lesson.

"*A-bu-ra*!"

"*A-bu-ra*!"

After half a month of this, Brother Ah Mao finally told them:

"*Abura* means oil."

"Teacher! Please continue to the next part of the lesson!"

"You stupid swine! How could I teach faster?"

His bellowing reduced the students to silence.

Suddenly one student stood up.

"Teacher! You're supposed to be a gentle guide. You shouldn't be cursing us like this."

"No way! Last month you brought me rice but no charcoal briquettes, so I had to eat the rice raw. You'd better believe I've got something to curse about. This month, since you brought me oil, my belly has gotten a bit more slippery, but I'm still eating raw rice. If you want me to turn over a new leaf and stop cursing, that's easy enough: next month, each of you bring me one picul of charcoal briquettes! Then, I can teach you another new lesson."

"Alright, then. Teacher, we don't feel we need to wait until next month; we'll bring the charcoal briquettes tomorrow. Please start teaching us how to say 'charcoal briquette' today!"

"You want me to teach you 'charcoal briquette' today?"

"Yes!"

"That'd be tricky!"

"Why?"

Brother Ah Mao was in an awkward spot.

"Because Japan doesn't have charcoal briquettes. Yesterday I took one to ask a Japanese person but he didn't know what they were called either. I'll have to look into it further, so let's still hold off on learning it until next month."

* * *

The following month, the "Japanese School" sign had disappeared from above Li Ah Mao's door, and in its place was a piece of paper with the following written on it:

*Seeking charcoal briquettes.*
*Will trade rice or cooking oil.*

***

## L. SEEKING LIFELONG PARTNER

The rice and oil Li Ah Mao had swindled through his Japanese school sustained him for two or three months until, once again, he found himself with his "pockets inside out." Just as he was thinking over what to do, Brother Ah Yang showed up.

"Brother Ah Mao! Have you come up with a new plan?"

"I've got a plan alright, but it requires the use of your honorable wife." Ah Mao giggled.

"If there's a buck in it, my wife is willing to do her bit."

Brother Ah Mao shook hands with Brother Ah Yang. "Thanks. In that case, go rent two P.O. boxes at the post office. Here's ten bucks."

"What do we need P.O. boxes for?" Brother Ah Yang asked in surprise.

"Don't worry about that. Just do as I say."

Brother Ah Yang agreed and took the ten dollars.

The next day, the following advertisement appeared in the *Shun Pao* newspaper:

## Rich Widow Seeks Lifelong Partner

*Beautiful, rich widow, age twenty-four, has for two years been bereft of her husband, from whom she inherited a large fortune. Still childless, she is eager to choose a mate with whom to start a family, and is seeking an unmarried man under the age of forty to be her lifelong companion. After marriage, she is willing to provide funds for her husband to develop a business. Sincere applicants are requested to send a letter and recent photograph to P.O. Box 606. Suitable candidates will be contacted by letter to arrange an in-person chat. Unsuitable candidates will not receive a reply.*

Seeing the advertisement, Brother Ah Yang asked Brother Ah Mao, "What kind of mysterious ruse is this? Where are you going to find a rich widow to meet the candidates if people actually apply?"

"That's why I want to employ your honorable wife!"

"You're putting a curse on me! I'm not dead, so how can the lady of my house become a widow?"

"If we don't call her a rich widow, would anyone fall for it? Dummy!"

That evening, Brother Ah Yang brought a stack of letters back from the post office and the two plunged into the work of sorting them.

Brother Ah Mao prepared a template for a reply letter and had Brother Ah Yang and his wife help copy it out. The letter read:

*I have received your honorable letter and photograph, which are very much to my liking. My parents, unfortunately, are both old fuddy-duddies and worry that I, a mere woman, might be easily tricked since I have no experience in choosing a husband. As such, I would like to invite you to meet for a short chat. On such-and-such a day at such-and-such an hour, please go to the*

*South China Tea House and wait to be received by my elder brother, who will recognize you by your honorable photograph.*

The content of each reply letter was exactly the same, except for the meeting times, which were staggered.

* * *

Early the next morning, Brother Ah Mao headed to the South China Tea House. Ah Yang's wife, made up beautifully as the bogus rich widow, accompanied him. They sat down at two tables set up some distance apart from each other and waited for the suitors to arrive.

The clock struck ten. According to the schedule, the first applicant should be arriving. As Brother Ah Mao watched the door, sure enough, a man wearing a fedora hurried in.

Brother Ah Mao pulled out a photograph and checked it against the man's face.

"Over here, Mr. Zhao!" he called out to him.

Embarrassed, Mr. Zhao sat down.

Brother Ah Mao reached into his wallet and handed the man a name card, on which was printed:

*Shanghai Charitable Relief Association*
*Mao Aili, Director*

"Honored to make your acquaintance!" Mr. Zhao smiled, offering the usual formalistic greeting.

Brother Ah Mao subtly gestured toward Mrs. Yang sitting in the corner: "That beautiful woman with the braided hair over there is my younger sister."

Mr. Zhao glanced over and spotted the elegantly made-up rich widow. She was a beauty indeed, and his heart skipped a beat.

Brother Ah Mao flattered Mr. Zhao with a few compliments and then chatted with him about issues related to proper social conduct. Finally, he turned to the matter at hand:

"These past few years I've been devoting my energies to charitable activities, and my sister has also been a tremendous help. Recently, we've been recruiting donors for a campaign to give gruel and alms to the poor. Our goal is five hundred thousand dollars. My sister and I have each donated twenty thousand, and we're now preparing to solicit donations from family and friends. If you'd be willing to give something, the amount doesn't matter. It would be a meritorious work of the highest order."

As he spoke, he pulled out a donations register.

"Forgive my presumption, today being our first meeting. It's most unreasonable of me to put you to any expense. That said, we'll be relatives before long—how about I just put you down for ten dollars? It's not much, and it'll make a good impression on my sister."

Mr. Zhao thought to himself: *This donation thing might be a smokescreen, and their real goal is probably to gauge my conscience. Fortunately, the amount's not much.*

As such, he replied with a show of munificence. "By all means! I'm always first in line when it comes to charity work."

Mr. Zhao was followed by Mr. Qian, and Mr. Qian by Mr. Sun. Some gave ten dollars; others sought to curry favor by donating greater amounts. In one day, Brother Ah Mao made over one hundred dollars. The next day they moved to a different location and raked it in.

After two weeks of activity, Brother Ah Mao did some calculations: they had received one hundred and forty applicants, ten per day, grossing a total of 2,450 dollars. Subtracting the costs of the P.O. boxes, the advertisement, stamps, and the fake diamond jewelry for Brother Ah Yang's wife, which totaled 250 dollars, they had cleared 2,200 dollars. Brother Ah Mao and the Yangs split the proceeds evenly, leaving them 1,100 dollars each. That night, they threw a celebratory banquet.

"In addition to making money, I haven't had to do any cooking for two weeks. I've gotten to eat barbecued pork dumplings and Cantonese-style rice, while those good-for-nothings fought to pick up the bill," Ah Yang's wife beamed. "Now that's what I call doing business!"

*   *   *

Those applicants who fantasized about marrying a rich widow, meanwhile, stopped receiving letters. Some went to the post office to look into the matter, only to discover that the rental period for the P.O. box had expired and that it was being used by a new customer.

***

# FARCES

# The Devil Messenger

## *A Farce*

DRAMATIS PERSONAE

Ah Ba, a carpenter
Wang Jinhu, a costume shop assistant
Qiu Shunquan, a landlord's accountant
Ten or more Delivery Men

*The stage set represents the interior of a broken-down room. On the left is a door. Ah Ba is in the room talking to himself.*

Ah Ba:

Ai! Now that the New Year's here, everyone is welcoming the God of Fortune.[1] So lively! (*Lowers his head and thinks.*) Now just wait a minute. Every single year, I've welcomed the God of Fortune too, but he's never visited me once. Instead of getting rich, the more I've welcomed him the poorer I've gotten. Every New Year's I'm harder up than last year, and each time I pray to him I end up poorer for my efforts. This year I'm going to try something different. If welcoming the God of Fortune won't bring me fortune, I might as well try welcoming the God of Misfortune. Forget the God of Fortune—bring on the King of Hell! Who knows? Maybe he'll actually help me get rich. Yep, that's what I'll do.

1. "Welcoming the God of Fortune" is a homecoming ceremony traditionally held on the fifth day of the Lunar New Year.

*Wang Jinhu has snuck in to eavesdrop on this monologue.*

WANG JINHU:

That Ah Ba is an odd one: instead of welcoming the God of Fortune, he welcomes the God of Misfortune. Gutsy! I'll dress up as a devil and scare the heck out of him.

*Exit Wang.*
*Ah Ba lights incense and candles and prays.*
*Enter Wang, in costume as a demon.*

AH BA:

Yikes!

WANG:

You must be Ah Ba.

AH BA:

I am, I am. Ah Ba's my name. What's yours?

WANG:

I am a devil messenger from the netherworld. Today is the fourth night of the New Year and everyone is welcoming the God of Fortune, while you alone are welcoming the King of Hell. The King can't come visit you personally, so you'll have to go to him. His Majesty sent me here to escort you thither.

AH BA:

Ah!

WANG:

You were fated to live a long life, but ever since you decided to make overtures to His Majesty, the King has had you on his mind.

He's decided that you'll draw your last breath tonight at midnight. Be prepared!

*Exit Wang.*

Ah Ba:

Yikes! Cripes! How could I die so young? I thought that if I welcomed the King of Hell he'd make me richer. I never thought he'd take my life instead! Now that the hour of my death is fixed, what else is there to say? (*Looks around.*) He said I'd draw my last breath at midnight. I don't have many hours to live. I don't want to die just like that, but at least after I die I won't have any more responsibilities. I might as well have myself some good wine and food before I go.

*8:00 pm.*

Ah Ba:

It's eight o'clock now. I think I'll go out and buy a few things on credit.

*Exit Ah Ba.*
*Enter the landlord's accountant, Qiu Shunquan.*

Qiu:

Anyone here? Is Ah Ba home? He's never home! But there're candles lit, so he couldn't have gone far. I'll wait for him a while.

*Enter Ah Ba.*

Qiu:

Ah Ba, where have you been? It's dangerous to leave candles lit when you go out.

Ah Ba:

Big deal. A broken-down place like this wouldn't be missed if it burned to the ground.

Qiu:

See, with an attitude like that, it's no wonder you're never willing to pay the rent you owe. Ah Ba, I came here tonight to collect the rent.

Ah Ba:

Say no more. I, Ah Ba, am not one to let my rent go unpaid. I'm five months behind, right?

Qiu:

That's right.

Ah Ba:

Tonight I can pay you for the last five months of rent and even prepay next month's.

Qiu:

Even next month's?

Ah Ba:

Don't underestimate me. I, Ah Ba, am not one to owe someone rent.

Qiu:

Pay up, then, if you're such a big spender.

Ah Ba:

I can't pay you just now, but I guarantee I'll give it to you at half past midnight.

Qiu:

Hey now! You're always making promises and then breaking them. You've set me up a hundred times, and now you want me to meet you at half past midnight? That's even more suspicious. No good, no good. You have to pay up now.

Ah Ba:

Why can't you get it through your head, you old dotard? I'm no deadbeat.

Qiu:

What's that?

Ah Ba:

(*With a smug look.*) See: who's the big spender now?

*Several Delivery Men come in, one after another.*

Delivery Man A:

Your ten liters of premium Shaoxing wine are here!

Delivery Man B:

Your three plates of shrimp-fried noodles are here!

*Both exit; enter two more Delivery Men.*

Delivery Man C:

Banquet dishes for two are here!

Delivery Man D:

Is this the place that ordered the four-dollar-per-table set menu?

*Both exit; enter two more Delivery Men.*

Delivery Man E:

Your fruit is here!

Delivery Man F:

Your tea snacks are here!

*Both exit.*

Ah Ba:

What do you think, Mr. Accountant? I'll give it to you straight: the God of Fortune himself is going to pay a visit here tonight. At midnight he's going to bring me ten thousand dollars!

Qiu:

Wow! Ten thousand dollars! Really?

Ah Ba:

What do you mean, "really?" Come here at midnight yourself if you don't believe me.

Qiu:

So, you've really hit the jackpot.

Ah Ba:

That's why you don't need to worry about your rent money. I'll pay you at half past midnight. If you've got money on you, lend me some now and I'll pay you back double: ten bucks for five, twenty for ten, and forty for twenty—or one thousand for a hundred, how about that?

Qiu:

So, you'll pay me ten dollars if I lend you five—double the money?

AH BA:

Forget double the money—I could even triple or quadruple it.

QIU:

Here's five dollars, then.

AH BA:

Better make it ten.

QIU:

Here's ten, then.

AH BA:

Twenty would be even better.

QIU:

Okay, twenty.

AH BA:

How about thirty, then?

QIU:

Alright, alright! Stop upping the ante. I'll lend you thirty dollars, and you'll pay me back sixty.

AH BA:

At half past midnight, you'll have your sixty dollars for sure.

QIU:

Half past midnight—that's the middle of the night. I'll just come by get it tomorrow morning. Fifteen dollars in rent plus a thirty-dollar loan comes to forty-five dollars, times two equals ninety dollars.

Ah Ba:

Ninety dollars is a hard figure to remember. Let's make it an even hundred.

Qiu:

One hundred, then. Thanks! I'll be by tomorrow morning.

Ah Ba:

Don't worry.

*Exit Qiu, delighted.*

*Ah Ba gets roaring drunk.*

Ah Ba:

Whaddaya know—I took him for a thirty-dollar funeral offering. What a surprise he'll get tomorrow morning! Too bad I won't get to see his face. These thirty bucks will come in handy. I've heard that everything in the netherworld costs money.

*A coffin is delivered from the coffin shop.*

Delivery Man G:

We've brought our "everlasting life" products.

Ah Ba:

Bring it in.

*The coffin is carried into the room.*

Delivery Man G:

Everything's inside.

Ah Ba:

Great. Come back for payment tomorrow morning.

DELIVERY MAN G:

As you wish. See you tomorrow.

*Exit Delivery Man G.*

*Ah Ba lies down in the coffin and then abruptly sits back up.*

AH BA:

This is actually a pretty comfy way to sleep. I wonder what time it is now.

*The faint sound of a clock striking eleven is heard.*

AH BA:

Gosh, it's already eleven. I'd better get ready.

*He takes out various objects.*

AH BA:

It's too hard in here. I need a mattress.

*Puts a mattress in the coffin.*

AH BA:

Time to put on my burial outfit.

*Shakes the wine pitcher next to him.*

AH BA:

Plenty left! And here's another plate of stir-fried shrimp. Might as well bring them in.

*Ah Ba closes the lid of the coffin over himself. After resting for a while, he pushes it open again.*

Ah Ba:

It's almost midnight. Why aren't I dead yet?

*He lets go of the coffin cover, which bonks him on the head.*

Ah Ba:

Ouch! Why aren't I dead yet?

*The clock strikes twelve.*

Ah Ba:

It's midnight. Time to close my eyes forever.

*He hurriedly closes the coffin lid. A moment later, the sound of snoring is heard.*

*The curtain comes down briefly and then rises again. The sun is now high in the sky, and sunlight shines into the room. The Delivery Men and Qiu Shunquan simultaneously arrive at the door to the shack.*

Qiu Shunquan:

Good morning! Ah Ba—not up yet? Ah Ba!

*Ah Ba, awakened by their noise, pushes open the coffin lid and stretches both hands in the air, yawning. He then scrambles to his feet and the coffin lid falls to the ground. Ah Ba looks around.*

Ah Ba:

Oh no!—I didn't die! (*Feels his own body.*) I'm really not dead. Why did that devil messenger last night trick me?

Delivery Man A:

Time to pay up for the wine!

Delivery Man B:

Time to pay up for the noodles!

Delivery Man C:

Hey there! Time to pay up for the banquet dishes!

Delivery Man D:

Time to pay up for the dishes from the Zhengyuan Restaurant!

Ah Ba:

Crap! If I'm not dead, then I owe all of them. What to do? (*Thinks for a minute, and then suddenly appears satisfied.*) I've got it: I'll pretend to be dead. (*Closes the coffin lid over himself again.*)

*The callers outside kick up a fuss.*

Qiu:

What do you all think? We've been hollering for a while and still haven't heard a peep from him. Do you think Ah Ba bolted during the night? We'd better force our way in.

ALL:

That's right! Let's do it!

*They force open the door and enter the room.*

Qiu:

Yikes! Why is there a coffin here?

*The creditors hurry over to the coffin. Opening the lid, they all recoil in shock.*

Qiu:

How horrible! Ah Ba's dead! How did this happen? He bought his own coffin—could he have committed suicide?

*Ah Ba sits up.*

Ah Ba:

Listen up, all of you.

All:

Woah!

*The creditors all fall to their knees.*

Ah Ba:

Now hear this: Last night, a devil messenger came at midnight and spirited me, Ah Ba, away to the netherworld, where I will reside hereafter. Old Mr. Qiu, I have a task for you. Come here.

Qiu:

Yikes!

Ah Ba:

The five months' rent plus the thirty dollars you lent me last night—forty-five dollars altogether—strike it from your account book, or else I'll put a curse on your family. We'll call it a funeral donation.

Qiu:

I will. Just don't haunt me!

Ah Ba:

Begone! The rest of you, come here.

All:

Yes.

Ah Ba:

Everything I owe for the things you delivered last night—strike them from the books or I'll come haunt your families.

ALL:

We will, we will! We promise. Don't put a curse on us!

AH BA:

In that case, I have something else for you to do. Old Mr. Qiu, you listen up too. I was a single man and have no surviving relatives to make offerings to my spirit. Pity me! You were fated from your previous incarnations to perform the funeral rites for me, so I must impose on you.

ALL:

What do you want us to do?

AH BA:

Old Mr. Qiu, you still owe me a condolence gift: five silver dollars and a set of new clothes will do it. Noodle-shop Owner, whip me up two plates of chicken chow mein and one foreign dollar. You, from the Wan Jia Xiang Restaurant, bring me a curry chicken over rice and one foreign dollar. Wineshopkeeper, gimme twenty liters of Shaoxing wine and one foreign dollar. You, from the Zhengyuan Restaurant, bring me a bowl of braised meatballs and one foreign dollar. You, from the Canton Snack Shop, bring me a stir-fried beef with onions and one foreign dollar. You, from the Longevity Funereal Shop, fetch me a pair of new shoes and two foreign dollars. You only have to provide me all these things for this evening; tomorrow you can take them all back. If you refuse to bring them, don't be surprised if your entire family dies, young and old alike.

ALL:

We'll do it! We'll do it!

*Just then, Wang Jinhu sneaks in and spies on this exchange.*

Ah Ba:

Since you've promised, leave now and bring me what I asked for.

All:

We will.

*They all flee out the door. Ah Ba comes out of the coffin.*

Ah Ba:

So stuffy in there! But it's all good. So the King of Hell can make me rich after all! I'm getting hungry. Why aren't they back with my food yet?

*Ah Ba smokes a cigarette. Hearing the sound of people talking outside, he hurriedly gets back into the coffin. Delivery Men bring food in, one by one, and place it on the table before scurrying off. Ah Ba periodically pokes his head out from the coffin to count the food items.*

Ah Ba:

Why hasn't Old Qiu shown up?

*Enter Qiu, carrying a package of clothing, which he places in the room before running off.*

Ah Ba:

It's all here. I'll take the money first—twelve bucks! Added to the forty-two I got last night, this is the most money I've ever had in my life. Now I can go back to my hometown and live like a king! This clothing's nice too; Old Qiu really put himself out on this one. (*Dons the funeral clothes.*) Now that I've got my duds on, I can have a good drink!

*Ah Ba gets drunk. Hearing someone outside, Ah Ba jumps back into the coffin in a panic. Enter Wang Jinhu, dressed as a devil messenger.*

Wang:

Ah Ba.

Ah Ba:

Yikes! You're that devil messenger from last night. What've you been fooling about? You said I was going to breathe my last at midnight last night. I almost died waiting!

Wang:

I came a little late and you were already asleep. I thought it would be a shame to spirit you away like that, and before I knew it, it was daybreak.

Ah Ba:

So, you're here to take me away now?

Wang:

That's right. Are you prepared to die?

Ah Ba:

You're joking! What young person wants to die? It was the same last night. If you can save me, I'll do whatever you want.

Wang:

If you don't want to die, naturally we can talk it over. Things work the same in the netherworld as in the human world: if you have money, give me half and I won't take you away.

Ah Ba:

You'll give me my life if I give you half my money? Thank you!

It was you who helped me get all this anyway, so here's half for you. (*He comes out of the coffin.*) Half comes to twenty-one dollars. Here, take it.

WANG:

Sorry to trouble you. So, what are you going to do now, Ah Ba?

AH BA:

Since I learned that I was going to die, I stuffed myself on food I got on credit. Then, wouldn't you know it, I didn't die, so there's no way I can go on living here. Better to get as far away from here as I can.

WANG:

That's right. You'd better beat it if you've snatched so much money and other stuff from people.

AH BA:

The food's getting cold. Eat up.

WANG:

Thanks.

*The two of them get roaring drunk and sing boisterously. Wang Jinhu forgets that he is in disguise and takes off his mask and costume.*

AH BA:

Hey! Aren't you Wang Jinhu?

*Wang Jinhu, startled, puts his costume back on.*

WANG:

Say what? I'm a devil messenger.

Ah Ba:

You dare trick me?! You even came to extort money from me. Ridiculous!

*Ah Ba makes to hit Wang.*

Wang:

Hold on a minute. Who helped you get money and fill your belly? How would you have gotten all this without me?

Ah Ba:

When you put it like that, you've got a point. I won't thump you, then.

Wang:

That's more like it. You owed me to begin with, so splitting the loot evenly is just the thing to do. Didn't you say just now that you plan to get out of here?

Ah Ba:

That's right.

Wang:

Ah Ba, I'm up to my neck in debt too. The boss fired me and I'm just living in his shop temporarily. I have to leave too, so we might as well skip town together.

Ah Ba:

Great! We'll go together. We'll be able to figure out things easier this way.

Wang:

Thanks. Let's get out of here before they come back.

Ah Ba:

It would be a shame to leave all this food uneaten. Relax! Let's finish it first and then split. There's plenty of time.

Wang:

Works for me!

*They gorge themselves.*

*The group of creditors reenter.*

Qiu:

Hey! Ah Ba isn't dead!

Delivery Man A:

He's drinking wine with Wang Jinhu.

All:

We've been duped! We won't let them off this time!

*They make to burst in.*

Qiu:

Hold on. I've got an idea.

*Qiu Shunquan intentionally stomps his feet loudly so that Ah Ba can hear.*

Ah Ba:

Someone's coming! (*Scrambles back into the coffin.*)

Wang:

Ah Ba, you've got somewhere to hide, but what about me?

Ah Ba:

You come in too. There's plenty of room for two.

Wang:

Great, great!

*The two get into the coffin and close the lid. Qiu Shunquan watches from the door.*

Qiu:

Good. Let's go in.

*The creditors enter the room.*

Qiu:

Poor Ah Ba. He died so young! (*Qiu winks at the others. Two or three of them come over and nail the coffin shut.*) Hurry and carry this outside the city walls and bury it.

Wang and Ah Ba:

Spare us! Spare us! Don't bury us!

All:

Did you hear a voice? Nope. We've gotten rattled and started hearing things. Carry it out!

Wang and Ah Ba:

No! We'll suffocate in this coffin! Help!

All:

You're in the coffin? Don't worry, you're young—too young to die!

Wang and Ah Ba:

We'll die for sure! Take off the lid, quick!

All:

Ha ha! We aren't afraid of you putting a curse on us anymore!

*Curtain.*

# A Father's Duty

## *A One-Act Farce in Three Scenes*

DRAMATIS PERSONAE

Kway See Chen, father
Dandy Chen, son
Dahlia, prostitute
Clothing Shop Assistant
Pearly, maidservant
Three or four friends and family
Two wedding attendants accompanying the newlyweds

### ACT I | SCENE ONE
**In Front of the Door to a Brothel**

*Enter Kway See Chen from the right, carrying a briefcase.*

Kway See:

Dahlia's probably been waiting for me a long time. I'd better hurry over and cheer her up with a visit.

*Smiling, he heads for the door of the brothel, when suddenly his son, Dandy Chen, enters from the left.*

Dandy:

Yikes, it's dad!

Kway See:

Huh? Dandy!

Dandy:

Where're you headed, father?

Kway See:

I … I'm just heading that way.

Dandy:

Where to?

Kway See:

Just the … you know—the bank!

Dandy:

The bank?

Kway See:

That's right, the bank. Where're you going?

Dandy:

I'm … to …

Kway See:

Where?

Dandy:

You know the soy sauce shop up ahead? Past the soy sauce shop's the pawn shop, and past that's a silk shop. Next to the silk shop there's a noodle house that's been making some great stuff recently.

Kway See:

I'm not asking you who makes great noodles. I want to know where you're going.

Dandy:

You want to know where I'm going?

Kway See:

I want to know where you're going.

Dandy:

Then *that's* where I'm going.

Kway See:

What?

Dandy:

I'm going to Old Zhang the Third's house.

Kway See:

So that's where you're going. Off you go, then. Don't loiter about here all day, and don't stay out too long.

Dandy:

Same for you, father. Head home once you're done with your errand.

*Both surreptitiously peek inside the brothel door as they walk off-stage in different directions. A moment later, Dandy reenters and looks around.*

Dandy:

Running into the old man really held me up.

*He is about to enter the brothel when Kway See suddenly reenters.*

Kway See:

What're you still doing here?

Dandy:

I … I was walking along when I ran into Old Zhang the Third's mother, who told me that he's not home, so I'm heading back home.

Kway See:

Don't hang about here, then. Off with you!

Dandy:

I'm off. But, dad, did the bank move or something?

Kway See:

No. I just decided that I can go to the bank tomorrow. I came back here because I've got something else to do today.

Dandy:

Well, once you're finished, don't you stay out too long either.

*Father and son once again head off in opposite directions. After two or three steps, both look back at the other.*

Kway See:

Back home with you!

Dandy:

Don't stay out long!

*Both exit. A moment or later, Kway See reenters and looks around him.*

Kway See:

Never thought I'd run into that little bastard and get tied up with his annoying prattle. What a pain!

*He is about to enter the brothel when Dandy reenters.*

Dandy:

Dad!

Kway See:

What the … ? —what're you doing back here again?

Dandy:

I was thinking that since I was already in the neighborhood I might as well go take a look at the exhibition hall. Dad, you must be done with that errand of yours, right?

Kway See:

I decided to deal with it tomorrow.

Dandy:

Then you might as well head home now.

Kway See:

You too. Come home as soon as you're done at the exhibition hall.

*They again head off in opposite directions. Dandy glances behind him and slips into the door to the brothel when his father isn't looking. Kway See glances back.*

Kway See:

Good, he's gone. I'd better go in while I can.

*He hurries inside the brothel. Scene change.*

## SCENE TWO
### Inside the Prostitute's Boudoir

*Setting: Dahlia's room.*

*Dandy is having a serious talk with Dahlia.*

Dahlia:

So you went home and started negotiating. Tell me quickly: how'd it go?

Dandy:

Perfectly. I brought it up with my father as soon as I got home yesterday. His first question was what kind of girl I wanted to marry.

Dahlia:

Yes.

Dandy:

I told him that she's an incomparable beauty, and that her family's status is a good match for ours. I told him that she's a twenty-year-old girl called Beautiful Maiden, and that she'll bring a dowry of three thousand dollars.

Dahlia:

Yes.

Dandy:

You know as well as I do that my old man loves money more than life itself. He was delighted and told me that I should marry her for sure.

Dahlia:

I'm so happy!

DANDY:

Now, as for the three thousand dollars and the rest of dowry, we'll follow the plan we discussed. As luck would have it, dad's here today—you can use your talents to finagle the money from him. He'll never guess you're doing it for me, and you'll be doing me a big favor. It's all up to you.

DAHLIA:

Don't worry. I promise you success.

*Just then, Pearly runs in, in a panic.*

PEARLY:

We're in trouble! Old Chen's mad that you haven't received him yet and is going to barge his way in here!

DAHLIA:

He's coming here? What about Young Master Chen, then?

DANDY:

Yeah, what about me!?

*Both are thrown into a panic.*

DANDY:

If dad hadn't raised me so big, I'd hide in a drawer.

DAHLIA:

Don't joke.

*The three of them are at a loss for what to do. Dahlia thinks for a moment.*

Dahlia:

I know what to do, though you'll find it a bit stuffy: hide in this wardrobe.

Dandy:

Alright, then. It's all up to you now.

Dahlia:

Don't you worry.

*Dandy climbs into the wardrobe.*
*Enter Kway See.*

Kway See:

What's the meaning of keeping me waiting like this? You know how I feel about you, but you never came out to receive me!

Dahlia:

I'm so sorry. Please, please forgive me! I was getting anxious too, but I couldn't do anything about it. It was the worst! I had to keep you waiting while I was tied up with some guest who can't take a hint. Just imagine! My body might have been with him, but my whole heart was yearning for a *tête-a-tête* with you. (*Pretends to cry.*)

Kway See:

It's my fault. I'm not really mad. Don't cry. I know how you feel about me. Nothing could have kept us apart today. There's no need to cry!

Dahlia:

Old Chen, you're so good to me! Just the sight of your smile fills me with joy. (*Snuggles up to Kway See.*)

Kway See:

Just the sight of my face makes you happy? Really?

Dahlia:

Like I've taken an energy-booster.

Kway See:

Looking at your face is like eating a cup of ice cream. Ha ha ha ha!

Dahlia:

Old Chen, a few days ago you said that you'd make me your wife. Why haven't you brought it up again since then?

Kway See:

I haven't forgotten! Everything will be ready soon. I just need two or three more days.

Dahlia:

I'm so happy!

Kway See:

I need a few more days because we've had a lucky break. And just what might that be, you ask? I have a son, and it might be somewhat unseemly if I were to marry you before he's married off.

Dahlia:

That's true.

Kway See:

Fortunately, my son's found a girl he likes. He became engaged to her of his own accord, which means he's set on marrying her.

Dahlia:

So that's it.

Kway See:

This is our chance, I thought, so I've been pushing him to get married in the next couple days. Once he's married, I can marry you. I hope you can endure waiting another two or three days.

Dahlia:

That's wonderful ... that means that in less than five days I'll be a member of your family.

Kway See:

That's right, that's right.

Dahlia:

But Old Chen, I have a request.

Kway See:

What's that?

Dahlia:

I have to make preparations too. I need to get some clothes made.

Kway See:

Say no more. I know just what your little heart desires.

Dahlia:

Is that so? I love you so much, Old Chen! But I can't make preparations just for myself.

Kway See:

Who needs to make preparations besides you?

Dahlia:

My husband!

Kway See:

I've got plenty of clothing already.

Dahlia:

When I marry you, we'll be newlyweds. We can't have people laughing at us behind our backs because one of us is old and the other's young. So, please, Old Chen, please don't wear old clothes. Have a new suit made.

Kway See:

That sounds reasonable. In that case, I'll have some clothes made for me.

Dahlia:

I'll telephone the tailor, then.

Kway See:

No need to be in such a rush.

Dahlia:

If we wait there won't be enough time.

*Exit Dahlia, happily. Pearly brings in wine and dishes. A moment later, Dahlia reenters.*

Dahlia:

I called the tailor and he'll bring some sample fabrics right over. Have a drink. (*She pours wine.*) I never imagined that at my age I'd be able to get married and become a proper wife.

Kway See:

You will.

Dahlia:

But I still have one more request.

Kway See:

There's more?

Dahlia:

My whole heart wants to marry you, but my body still owes money—three thousand dollars altogether. What to do about this?

Kway See:

What? Three thousand! So much! That's as much as my daughter-in-law's dowry.

Dahlia:

What?

Kway See:

Never mind. Would a thousand dollars be enough to pay off your debt?

Dahlia:

If you're not willing, just forget it. The money's not for me anyway. Keep your thousand dollars. I guess I've misjudged you.

Kway See:

Don't get mad, Dahlia. Don't think I'm unwilling to pay up. Okay, okay, I'll give it to you.

Dahlia:

Really? Thank you so, so much! That's why I've always told people: Old Chen is no penny-pincher.

KWAY SEE:

You're not the only one who says so either. I've heard other people say the same thing.

DAHLIA:

That's right. Can you give me the money now, then, Old Chen?

KWAY SEE:

You're so impatient! I guess there's nothing for it but for me to give you the three grand now.

*Kway See takes out his checkbook and signs a check for three thousand dollars, which he hands to her. Pearly shows in the Clothing Shop Assistant.*

ASSISTANT:

I'm from the Shuntai Emporium. We received your phone call just now, and I've brought over a special delivery of sample fabrics for your inspection. Here you go. These colors here are perfect for a young lady of twenty or so who wants to make a splash, while these colors are most appropriate for a lad in his early twenties.

KWAY SEE:

(*Finding this odd.*) What? A lad in his early twenties?

DAHLIA:

That's right. These colors are all suitable for a lad in his early twenties.

KWAY SEE:

Dahlia, who's supposed to wear this young man's garb?

DAHLIA:

You! Since you're taking a young bride, you need to dress the part.

KWAY SEE:

That's true, but wouldn't a fifty-two or fifty-three-year-old man dressed up as a twenty-something seem a bit …

DAHLIA:

No way! When you're dressed up, I promise that you'll look like a dashing old gentleman. (*Lays a piece of cloth over his shoulder.*) A perfect match … Mr. Wang, doesn't he look like a twenty-something?

ASSISTANT:

You said it! Third Miss, you should use this fabric. (*Drapes a piece of cloth over Dahlia's shoulders. Dahlia and Kway See stand shoulder to shoulder, and the Assistant takes a step back to size them up.*) Every inch the bridal couple.

KWAY SEE:

Mr. Wang, do you think we're a good match?

ASSISTANT:

A match made in Heaven.

KWAY SEE:

Ha ha! In that case, Mr. Wang, please get right to work.

ASSISTANT:

Yes, sir. So, you've settled on these fabrics?

KWAY SEE:

You'll need to work fast.

Assistant:

They'll be done within five days, guaranteed.

*Exit Clothing Shop Assistant. A snore is heard from the wardrobe. Kway See jumps up in alarm and looks about.*

Kway See:

Someone's sleeping in here.

Dahlia:

(*Anxiously.*) Not in here, Old Chen. There's a guest sleeping in the room next door.

Kway See:

Sure sounds close.

Dahlia:

The sound was probably carried here on the wind.

Kway See:

That must be it. (*He listens for another moment and appears convinced.*) I had originally wanted to have a good, long chat with you today, but I have a lot of things to take care of, so I'll have to go home now.

Dahlia:

Why do you have to leave so soon? You haven't even sat long enough to warm your seat.

Kway See:

Please endure my absence for the time being. In just two or three days we can chat from morning till night. For now we'll just have to suffer a bit.

*Exit Kway See. Dahlia opens her wardrobe, in which the snoring continues.*

DAHLIA:

Come on, out you get.

DANDY:

Yaaaaaaaaaawn!

*He yawns and stretches for a moment, and then emerges from the wardrobe.*

DAHLIA:

Curse you! Such loud snoring—you scared the heck out of me.

DANDY:

I'm sorry. Has the old man gone?

DAHLIA:

He just left.

DANDY:

Ah, good. So, how did it go?

DAHLIA:

Excellent, excellent! I've got my dowry right here. (*Shows Dandy the check.*) I've ordered clothing for both of us too.

*Scene change.*

## SCENE THREE

### The Marriage Hall in the Chen Residence

*The host, Kway See Chen, paces about by himself.*

Kway See:

Everything's perfect! What luck that this daughter-in-law will be bringing in a three thousand dollar dowry. That'll be just enough for me to take a wife myself. Once today's wedding is over, tomorrow it'll be my turn. Perfect, perfect!

*The Guests enter all at once.*

All Guests:

Congratulations! Congratulations!

Kway See:

My deepest thanks to you all!

Guest A:

Uncle Chen, with a daughter-in-law joining the family, you won't have to worry about domestic matters any more.

Guest B:

It's already been ten years since Mrs. Chen passed away, hasn't it?

Guest C:

It's been hard on you, raising your son all by yourself. By bringing in a daughter-in-law, your father's duty will truly be complete, and you can finally pass off the responsibility for your son's care to her.

Guest D:

Now you can look for a nice, relaxing place in which to pass your old age.

GUEST E:

That way you can live out your waning years in comfort.

KWAY SEE:

You all mean to say, in other words …

GUEST A:

We all feel that this would be the best thing for you. You've really had it tough up to now. From now on you'd be best off turning over management of the shop to your son and focus on awaiting the arrival of your grandson.

GUEST B:

That's right! Finding a nice, relaxing place to live out your senior years is a great idea, but it'd be a bit lonely without someone to talk to. The best thing would be to find someone around your age whom you could really relate to. I brought it up with my old lady the day before yesterday, and I think I've found just the right woman for you.

ALL:

What's she like?

GUEST B:

She's got a great personality, and she's about the same age as Old Chen. She's a Buddhist to boot.

KWAY SEE:

This is going too far.

ALL:

No, really, she's perfect for you. Let us introduce her so you two can have a chat.

Kway See:

I, uh …

*Music. Enter the groom, Dandy Chen, and the bride, Dahlia, both wearing wedding finery. Kway See Chen looks first at Dandy's clothes.*

Kway See:

Strange.

*Kway See looks Dandy up and down.*

Kway See:

What a coincidence.

*He then goes over to the bride and examines her clothes.*

Kway See:

Her get-up is the same. Color's the same too. How bizarre.

Kway See *lowers his head and ponders.*

Dandy:

Father, are you unsure about something?

Kway See:

No, but I'm eager to take a look at the bride's face.

Dandy:

Let's take off her veil, then.

*Dandy removes Dahlia's veil.*

Kway See:

Good grief! It's you!

*Kway See's face goes pale from shock.*

DANDY:
Dad, do you recognize her?

KWAY SEE:
No, no.

*Dandy pulls out the check.*

DANDY:
Here's the bride's three thousand dollar dowry.

KWAY SEE:
Whaa! This is my money too …

DANDY:
What's that?

KWAY SEE:
Nothing.

DANDY:
My clothes were also provided by the bride's family.

KWAY SEE:
That was also my …

DANDY:
What's that?

KWAY SEE:
The bride's family had the clothes made too? Wonderful, wonderful!

Dandy:

You said it. Come over and meet father.

*Dahlia attentively curtsies to Kway See.*

Dahlia:

Father.

Kway See:

Alright, alright. Enough already.

*Friends and family are delighted.*

All:

And just like that, a father's duty is fulfilled!

*Curtain.*

# Marrying Indirectly

## *A One-Act Farce in Four Scenes*

DRAMATIS PERSONAE

Lechy Lao, a gentleman
Junior Lao, Lechy's son
Lao's Pal, Lechy's friend
Lao Family Servant
Tender Blossom Yang, a bride
Daddy Yang, Tender Blossom's father
Mommy Yang, Tender Blossom's mother
Yangs' Maidservant
Several wedding celebrants and musicians

### ACT I | SCENE ONE
### Mr. Lao's Study

*Lechy Lao wears a worried expression and holds his head in both hands. He then looks upward and lets out a long sigh.*

Lechy:

Ai … This is such a pitiless world! Heaven and earth are so cruel! Will my passionate feelings ever make their way into her heart?

*Enter Lao Family Servant.*

SERVANT:

Master, your dinner is ready.

LECHY:

Do I look like I want dinner? I don't want to eat a thing. Scram!

SERVANT:

The young master is concerned about you and insists that I see that you get something to eat.

LECHY:

I'm not interested. Don't come around bothering me.

SERVANT:

Really, the young master repeatedly insisted that I look after you.

LECHY:

I told you I'm not eating. What are you still doing here?

SERVANT:

Master, I specially selected your favorite dishes.

LECHY:

Damn it! Why don't you get the hell out of here!

*Lechy holds his head in his hands to shut him out, leaving the Servant no option but to withdraw.*

LECHY:

All this commotion is about to make my head explode!

*Lechy continues sitting and moping by his desk. Just then, Junior Lao returns from school.*

Junior:

Father, you're home.

*Lechy is annoyed at this intrusion too.*

Lechy:

You're back.

Junior:

Teacher Zhu is sick this afternoon, so my last class was cancelled and I came home early.

Lechy:

Go review your lessons, then.

Junior:

Tomorrow's Sunday. Why don't we have a chat instead? I wanted to ask you about this illness of yours …

*Lechy looks even more pained.*

Lechy:

I'm feeling terrible today. Please don't ask me anything.

*Lechy rests his head on his desk and is silent, leaving his son no option but to withdraw. Enter Lao's Pal.*

Pal:

Still haven't recovered yet, old pal? Cheer up! What's got you down?

LECHY:

Don't try to cheer me up. I'll be unhappy as long as I draw breath, and in the end I can only die of sorrow.

PAL:

Why so down? You're like a lovesick youth!

LECHY:

Hearing you say that breaks my heart even more.

PAL:

Well, I find that odd, Old Lech. Today I came to ask you a question. You've already seen several doctors about your illness, but none of them have been able to make head or tail of it, except to say that it seems like an illness that only afflicts the young. Elderly people never show these symptoms. But Dr. Wang says that the root of the problem is that you're preoccupied by something that you feel conflicted whether or not to talk about. Even your son's worried. The way I see it you'd be best off just telling me, your old buddy.

LECHY:

I'm ashamed to hear you say it. I do indeed have a weight on my mind, but it's one I can't even tell an old friend like you. All I can do is die!

PAL:

Stop kidding. What could possibly make you want to die? You're rich, you're famous, your son's about to graduate from university. Your one great misfortune is that your wife died early. Even then, she didn't die in her thirties or forties; she was over fifty when she passed away—and that can't be considered bad fortune. So I urge you not to be so depressed. Instead, you should hurry up and find yourself a new wife.

LECHY:

Old pal, what you say makes me want to die even more.

PAL:

What did I say that could make you want to die? This is bizarre! Whatever it is, you can tell me. If it's a secret, you can trust me to keep it. I won't let it slip, I promise.

LECHY:

Since you're so concerned, I'll just have to muster up the resolve to tell you. But don't you laugh at me!

PAL:

No one's going to laugh at you. Hurry up and tell me.

LECHY:

It happened a month ago when I took my son to an amusement hall ...

PAL:

Yes?

LECHY:

... when, to my surprise, along came a beautiful girl.

PAL:

Oh!

LECHY:

Don't laugh! That beautiful girl is the reason I'm so miserable today. Now you know why I want to die!

PAL:

No wonder everyone says you're a good man who always

thinks of others first. I never thought you'd be so attentive in choosing a daughter-in-law. This is a cause for happiness! How could you talk of dying? Hurry and explain things to your son to cheer him up. (*Makes to leave.*)

LECHY:

Where are you going?

PAL:

Since it's this daughter-in-law business that's gotten you down, shouldn't I go explain things to your son?

LECHY:

Not so fast. What do you mean "this daughter-in-law business"?

PAL:

What is it then?

LECHY:

It's embarrassing to talk about. I've fallen in love with someone I shouldn't.

PAL:

(*Shocked.*) What!? You?!

LECHY:

That's right. Instead of finding a wife for my son, I've become a wreck myself, and I can't face him. Love is indifferent to anything but itself, you see. I feel I've gotten my youth back. So take pity on your old pal and pull him out of the abyss. If you don't, I'll be a goner soon for sure!

PAL:

You really scared the heck out of me!

Lechy:

I don't blame you. This is the only favor I'll ever ask of you, old pal: do everything you can to help me think of a way to make this beautiful woman mine. If you won't save me, I'll die and become a lovelorn ghost.

Pal:

All right, all right. Which family is this beauty from, then?

Lechy:

That I don't know.

Pal:

How can you be in love with her if you don't even know her name?

*Enter Junior Lao.*

Junior:

Father, I overheard what you were saying just now. Why didn't you say something to me earlier? If I'd only known, you'd never have had to suffer so. Don't you worry about that girl; she'll be yours.

Lechy:

Son, I'm too ashamed to face you.

Pal:

Junior, do you know which family this girl is from?

Junior:

She's the daughter of the Yang family on Pebble Street, uncle.

Pal:

There! So that's where she's from. Lech, ol' buddy, leave it to me and set your mind at rest. I promise I'll put her in your hands.

LECHY:

In my hands? I'm so happy. (*Momentarily cheers up.*) I leave everything to you.

PAL:

In that case, let me go do some prospecting and then we'll talk again. (*Makes to leave.*)

JUNIOR:

Many thanks. (*Sees him out.*)

*Scene change.*

## SCENE TWO

### A ROOM IN THE YANG RESIDENCE

*Tender Blossom lies in bed.*

BLOSSOM:

Ai! Doesn't he know my feelings? The world is so heartless. Heaven and earth are so cruel. I want to die!

*Rests her head on the table. Enter Maidservant, carrying a glass of milk.*

MAID:

Have a glass of milk, miss.

BLOSSOM:

Do I look like I want a glass of milk?

Maid:

The master and mistress insisted that I bring this for you to drink.

Blossom:

I told you I don't want it. Didn't you hear me?

Maid:

Just take a sip.

Blossom:

I won't, I won't, I won't!

*Tender Blossom throws the glass of milk to the floor and goes into the next room.*

Maid:

Why is she so angry? What's got into her? Quite the demure young lady! Why is she acting like this?

*Maidservant straightens up the room and mops up the spilled glass of milk. Enter Daddy Yang and Mommy Yang.*

Daddy:

Did she drink a little?

Maid:

No—and she even broke the glass!

Mommy:

Broke it!?

Maid:

That's right.

MOMMY:

But why? She's such a good girl …

*The parents sit down.*

DADDY:

The doctor was right. He said she's harboring some secret.

MOMMY:

That must be it.

MAID:

Ma'am, in that case, let me go talk to her and get to the bottom of this.

MOMMY:

Who knows: maybe she'll be willing to confide in you. In that case, pretend that nothing is amiss and see what you can find out.

MAID:

Yes, ma'am. (*Exits.*)

*Husband and wife let out a long sigh. A moment later, the Maid returns, looking happy.*

MAID:

Master, mistress, don't worry: everything's clear now.

DADDY:

Everything's clear? What is it that has her so worried?

MAID:

Actually, she's not to be blamed for this.

Mommy:

She's not to be blamed? Tell us what's going on.

Maid:

Remember how I accompanied the young lady to the amusement hall a few days ago?

Daddy:

Yes.

Maid:

While we were there we saw a young man and his father.

Mommy:

You mean the father and son of the Lao clan?

Maid:

The same. As soon as miss saw the young master of the Lao clan …

Mommy:

The young master of the Lao clan?

Maid:

That's right. He's the root cause of her illness.

Mommy:

So that's it.

*Mommy and Daddy Yang are stunned.*

Mommy:

Now we know the cause of her illness, but as for the Lao clan … that's a tricky one.

DADDY:

That's a tricky one alright. If our two families were of equal status there would be something to talk about, but the Laos are so rich …

MOMMY:

They'd never agree to it. Even leaving aside their family status, my daughter's health is in danger. (*Looks left and right.*) She looks ready to die!

DADDY:

It's a tricky one. Didn't I tell you the other day that they shouldn't go out?

MOMMY:

How could I have known that something like this would happen?

DADDY:

We've got to think of something …

*Both lower their heads in thought. Reenter Maidservant.*

MAID:

There's a visitor outside who insists on seeing the mistress.

MOMMY:

Please show him in, then.

MAID:

Yes. (*Exits.*)

*Husband and wife straighten their clothing. Enter Lao's Pal.*

Pal:

Long time, no see.

Daddy:

So it's you.

Pal:

I've been sent here today to act as matchmaker.

Mommy:

Marriage!

Pal:

I'm here on behalf of the Lao clan. They're set on making a match with your daughter.

Mommy:

Really? The Laos are interested in our daughter! That's wonderful! Actually, my daughter has been so unhappy this past week that she's stopped eating. She's gotten so thin that when the doctor saw her he told us that she must have something on her mind. Later, we had the maidservant find out what was going on, and it turns out that it was about this …

Pal:

Indeed.

Mommy:

A few days ago I took my daughter to the amusement hall.

Pal:

That's right. And there you happened to bump into a delicate, fair-looking man. Ha ha!

Mommy:

So you already know about this? It was the Lao men after all.

Pal:

So your young miss took a liking to him and came down with lovesickness. Ha ha! Truly a marvelous match! Who knew that they would fall for each other like this. Since visiting the amusement hall, they've both been suffering from lovesickness.

Mommy:

So they're both in the same situation. We were just talking about sending someone over to the Lao residence for a chat, but we concluded that they were too far above our station. I can't think how delighted my daughter will be when I share your news with her. Wait while I go tell her.

*Mommy Yang is about to go in when Tender Blossom Yang rushes out.*

Blossom:

Mommy, I'm so happy! Uncle, thank you so much! Mr. Lao must think well of me if he's been at home suffering lovesickness too. You don't have to worry about my illness anymore, Mommy. I'm ready to start eating again.

Pal:

Truly a marvelous match! I never imagined that it would be sealed so quickly. I'll go report back to the Laos now and return in a few days. (*Exits, delighted.*)

Blossom:

Dad, Mom, I've heard that the Young Master of the Lao clan is an outstanding university student. You saw him, didn't you, Mommy? He's such a looker! Ha ha ha ha!

Daddy:

You're not the only one who's happy. His family's rich too. His father's a member of parliament!

Mommy:

For our daughter to marry into such a family will reflect great credit on us parents too.

*All three look delighted.*

*Scene change.*

## SCENE THREE
### The Marriage Hall

*Lechy and Tender Blossom exchange bows. Tender Blossom pulls aside her veil and, seeing Junior Lao standing in a corner of the room, rushes over to bow to him. Seeing his stepmother bow to him, Junior Lao hurriedly returns a lower bow to her. After several bows, Lechy suddenly sees that the bride has disappeared. Looking around, he spots her bowing in the corner and goes over to bow to her there. As Junior Lao repeatedly dodges, Tender Blossom chases him and Lechy chases her, each bowing all the time.*

Servant:

Whose bride is this, after all? It seems like she's the old master's, but it also appears like she's the young master's. I can't make head or tail of it.

*Scene change.*

## SCENE FOUR
### The Nuptial Chamber

*Tender Blossom is alone in the room.*

*Enter Lechy Lao.*

Blossom:

Please have a seat, Father.

Lechy:

I, uh … don't want to sit. You must be lonely, all alone in this room. They've got a magician outside. Why don't you go out to watch?

Blossom:

Thank you, I plan to stay here to watch over the maids and put away the clothing my husband changed out of.

Lechy:

My clothing?

Blossom:

No … my husband's.

Lechy:

That would be mine.

Blossom:

No, my husband's.

Lechy:

Well, then, finish your task soon. I'll be waiting for you outside.

Blossom:

Thank you.

*Exit Lechy. Enter Junior Lao.*

Blossom:

I was just about to call the maids to put away the clothing you changed out of.

Junior:

Thank you, Mother.

Blossom:

That's funny. Why are you calling me "mother"?

Junior:

It's only fitting.

Blossom:

What?

Junior:

I lost my mother when I was young, so I've never experienced maternal love. I hope you'll treat me like your own son, mother.

Blossom:

Ah! What is it you don't you like about me, teasing me like this? If there's really something wrong with me, just tell me straight out.

*The two converse. Enter Lechy.*

Lechy:

Ridiculous! You shameless slut!

BLOSSOM:

Father, how could you say a thing like that?! Why are you calling me a slut, Father?

LECHY:

You dare to ask me when you're cavorting with your husband's son right in front of him?

BLOSSOM:

You're wrong, Father. Any parents would be happy to see their son and daughter-in-law getting along so well. I've never done anything inappropriate with other people behind my husband's back.

LECHY:

Yikes! Didn't you come here to marry me?

BLOSSOM:

I came to marry your son and become your daughter-in-law.

JUNIOR:

Yikes! She's my wife!

LECHY:

Aiyo! She's my daughter-in-law! My old illness is back! (*Exits, holding his head.*)

*Curtain.*

# Upstairs, Downstairs: Two Couples

## *A One-Act Comedy in Three Scenes*

DRAMATIS PERSONAE

Mr. Shameless
Miss Parrot
Lucky, chauffeur
Happy, maid
Several friends, relatives, wedding musicians, and the like

### ACT I | SCENE ONE
### The Park

*Enter Lucky, looking behind him.*

Lucky:

That guy walking this way looks like our young master. Where could he be going at a time like this? I'll hide and watch what he does. (*He hides behind a tree.*)

*Enter Shameless, who sits on a bench and smokes a cigarette.*

*Enter Happy, also looking behind her.*

Happy:

Hey, that's our young mistress coming this way. Where could she be going at a time like this? I'll hide and watch what she does. (*She hides behind a tree.*)

*Enter Parrot, who sits next to Shameless. Shameless looks pleased, and produces a book.*

Shameless:

"A man and a fan." That's right. It says that rice is expensive in China right now. These foreign magazines have such detailed reporting! There's more: "A pen and a fan." It says that 13,293 people died in an earthquake in Italy.

*The two of them slowly draw closer to each other, back to back. Shameless takes Parrot's hand.*

Shameless:

Success, success.

Parrot:

Happy, so happy.

*They turn and face each other.*

Shameless:

Miss, the hand-holding that you and I performed just now was a most fervent one. Though driven by motives of the purest and most platonic nature, it most assuredly established our love for one another. Let us hasten to exchange names. I am an underclass college student at a superior university. My name is Shameless and I'm twenty-four years old.

Parrot:

My name is Parrot and I'm nineteen years old. My father is a military officer.

Shameless:

So you're nineteen and I'm twenty-four. Subtract our ages and we are but five years apart. Truly a jadelike pair. If only I could be with a beauty like you …

Parrot:

If only I could be with a handsome man like you …

Shameless:

Ha ha ha ha!

Parrot:

Ha ha ha ha!

Shameless:

So happy! Now we can swear a lover's oath: The seas may go dry and the mountains collapse, but our love will remain steadfast.

Parrot:

May it be so.

*They hold hands again.*

Shameless:

Now that both our hearts are resolved, we need only obtain our fathers' permission. My father is not at all strict about this sort of thing. He's never interfered with my marriage plans and has encouraged me to choose my own mate.

Parrot:

Mine too. My father's the same. Even though he's a military

officer he's quite open-minded. He's often chatted with me, his daughter, about how he believes in free love and modern-style courtship. So he's sure to accept the man I choose.

SHAMELESS:

Good, wonderful. That's just how fathers should be.

PARROT:

Indeed.

SHAMELESS:

Too many parents consider youthful passion to be the height of moral depravity and they suppress the good along with the bad. That's a big mistake. In any case, the passions of youth are physiological, a force of nature. Without the passions of youth, human life would be worthless. We'd be idiots, madmen. It's an explosive passion. If suppressed for no reason, there's sure to be negative repercussions. One's certain to fall into cynicism, or self-abandonment, or insanity.

PARROT:

Your esteemed views are entirely correct. Parents see romantic love between young people of a certain age as something to guard against. But if they repress it too severely, they'll dull their children's psychological development.

SHAMELESS:

That's right. We're both fortunate in this regard.

PARROT:

You said it.

SHAMELESS:

Miss Parrot, this place isn't convenient for an in-depth chat. Shall we repair to a fine restaurant nearby?

Parrot:

Okay.

*Exit Shameless and Parrot, holding hands.*

*Lucky comes out from behind his tree.*

Lucky:

Nice! Our young master is usually so well behaved. Who could have guessed he'd pull this sort of stunt?! He's got the skill, I must say. Then again, I'm a man myself. Wouldn't it be something if some day *I* wore a Western suit and walked hand-in-hand with a co-ed? (*Lowers his head thoughtfully.*) I'll take a page from the young master's book and find myself a co-ed to fool around with. But what'll I do without a suit? (*Thinks again.*) I know—I'll borrow one from the young master on the sly.

*Exits, elated. Happy emerges.*

Happy:

So that's what our young lady's been up to. And me thinking she's just a little girl! Here she's already found her own sweetheart. Now, I'm a woman myself. Why don't I put on her clothes and find me a sweetheart here too? (*Lowers her head thoughtfully.*) That's just what I'll do.

*Exit Happy.*

*Enter Lucky, dressed in a bizarre-looking Western suit and sporting a cane.*

Lucky:

I've got my suit and I've got my cane: now I'm a presentable young master myself! (*Sits down.*) If I wait here, some girl's bound to come by. (*Looks around.*)

*Enter Happy, wearing a horrendous outfit, who sits down beside Lucky. Each glances at the other out of the corner of an eye and smiles.*

LUCKY:

Whoops! I forgot Step Number One. (*Produces a book.*) "*Jili geluo, jili gulu, bili buluo.*" This foreign book says that rice in China is so expensive that chauffeurs can only afford to eat flatbread. "*Chicken chow fun, hotdog onna bun, five four three two one.*" It says that seventy-four-and-a-half people died in an earthquake in Italy.

*The two move closer to each other and hold hands.*

LUCKY:

Wonderful, wonderful.

HAPPY:

Lovely, lovely.

*They turn and face each other.*

LUCKY:

From which family does this young lady hail? When I held your hand just now, all three thousand six hundred pores on my skin burst open at once. Let me tell you who I am: I'm a third-year student at the ol' local university. My name's Shameless and I'm twenty-four years old.

HAPPY:

So that's who you are. I'm the daughter of the commander of the third battalion. My name's Parrot and I'm nineteen years old.

Lucky:

You're nineteen and I'm twenty-four. Bring us together and we're forty-three. What a happy couple!

Happy:

Like a pair of mandarin ducks.

Lucky:

Our love is deeper than a cesspool. Furthermore, my local temple god has always approved of me whoring around.

Happy:

My father's the same. Even though he's a military man, he's quite open-minded. He talks to me freely about how he believes that sweet rice should have lard added to make it more delicious.

Lucky:

Good, wonderful. That's just how fathers should be. But let's stop all this queer talk. Your tummy's rumbly, isn't it?

Happy:

Yes.

Lucky:

Let's go find some place to eat.

Happy:

Okay.

Lucky:

There's the Origins of Virtue Restaurant, but there are too many people there. Let's go to a nearby foreign restaurant instead.

I'm a regular there. The food's great. Shall we go together, Miss Parrot?

*The two exit, holding hands.*

## SCENE TWO
### The Restaurant

*One Diner is eating in the restaurant.*

*A waiter escorts Lucky and Happy in.*

WAITER:

Please have a seat. What would you like to eat?

LUCKY:

We want to drink something first. Bring me two liters of whiskey, and warm it up first.[1]

WAITER:

You might have come to the wrong place, sir. Were you hoping to eat Chinese food?

LUCKY:

I don't like Chinese food. I lived for four years in Fürerhausdifang, Germany, and I can't stand Chinese food anymore. Only foreign food will do.

1. Chinese wine and spirits were traditionally warmed before being served.

Waiter:

We have all kinds of foreign food here. What would you like?

Lucky:

That's no good. Back in Fürerhausdifang the customer didn't have to order dishes. He'd sit down and the wait staff would just bring out the food because they'd already know what he likes.

Waiter:

We don't do things that way here.

Lucky:

How do you do things then?

Waiter:

The customer places his order, and we can cook anything he wants.

Lucky:

So you can cook anything; tell me some dishes, then.

Waiter:

They're on the menu. Pick anything you like.

Lucky:

Wrong again! That's not the way they do it in Germany. They list their dishes on the menu too, but the waiter has to read all of them aloud. If you don't read them to me, how can I order?

Waiter:

That may be the way they do it in foreign countries, but not here in China. The customer has to read them himself, and to write out the ones he wants.

LUCKY:

What do people eat here, then?

WAITER:

The first course has to be soup.

LUCKY:

Why didn't you say so earlier? We'll have a blood soup or a guts soup.

HAPPY:

Let's have a winter melon and tofu soup.

WAITER:

We don't have stuff like that. We only have fancy dishes.

LUCKY:

Nonsense. If you don't even have simple stuff, how could you have fancy dishes? In that case, just bring whatever you want.

WAITER:

How about ox tail soup? The second course will be fish.

LUCKY:

Make it smoked fish—a small portion.

WAITER:

We don't have smoked fish. How about fried croaker? And perhaps a couple orders of pork *viande* or beef *viande*?

LUCKY:

Why not Burglar Brand or Great Wall Brand?

Waiter:

Those are cigarettes. I'll put you down for a couple of pork chops.

*Waiter brings their dishes over.*

Lucky:

After you.

Happy:

After you.

Lucky:

Don't be so polite.

Happy:

Don't be so polite either.

Lucky:

I'm going to have some wine first.

Happy:

Me too.

*The Diner at the table next to them is in the middle of his meal. The pair imitates how he uses knife and fork. The Diner notices them and is amused, so he starts purposefully misleading them. First he taps himself on the head with his fork, and the pair imitates him. Then he makes a circle in the air with his knife, and the pair imitates him again. Instead of cutting his large pork chop into smaller pieces, he pinches his nose with one hand and shoves the whole chop into his mouth with the other; the pair again imitates him. Having finished eating, the Diner stands up and begins to leave. When the pair stand up too, he laughs loudly and then exits.*

LUCKY:

He must be going home.

*They sit back down and continue eating. Enter the Waiter, escorting Shameless and Parrot. Lucky and Happy run away in a panic; Shameless and Parrot catch a glimpse of them as they exit.*

SHAMELESS:

What's going on? Those two customers were scared off by us all of a sudden.

PARROT:

Yes. That woman looked like our maid.

SHAMELESS:

She did. The man looked like my chauffeur too.

*They sit down and place their order with the Waiter, who then exits.*

SHAMELESS:

Miss Parrot, our marriage negotiations have succeeded!

PARROT:

Yes. A perfect outcome. Now we can set a date for the wedding.

*Lucky and Happy still stand at a corner of the stage.*

HAPPY:

Horrible! Yikes!

LUCKY:

Horrible! Yikes!

Parrot:

Look, that girl really is my family's maid. She's mimicking me, dressed up like that. I thought that something was up when she came in. So it turns out she's been fooling around here with a boyfriend.

Shameless:

So that's it. That man is my family's chauffeur. Look, he's all dressed up, imitating me. I also heard rumors that he'd been fooling around with someone outside the family. I never guessed it would turn out to be a maid from your household. Not a bad match.

Parrot:

Ha ha!

## SCENE THREE

### The Marriage Hall in the Groom's Household

*Seats are filled with relatives and friends. Shameless and Parrot are in the midst of the wedding ceremony. Suddenly Lucky enters and grabs Parrot.*

Lucky:

Parrot, how dare you take advantage of me! Didn't we get engaged that day in the park?

*Lucky berates Parrot, who is startled and bursts into tears. Enter Happy, who grabs Shameless.*

Happy:

You're so heartless, Shameless! I got engaged to you in the park; how could you go and marry someone else's daughter?

Shameless:

Let go of me! I don't know you.

Happy:

What do you mean you don't know me? Shameless, you're so cold-hearted. Didn't you tell me that day that you wanted to grow old with me?

*Happy looks up at him.*

Happy:

Yikes! This one's not really Shameless! (*She looks around and suddenly spots Lucky.*) *He's* really Shameless!

Lucky:

Hey, it's Parrot! Do you still love me?

*The two hold hands.*

All:

Another married couple!

*Curtain.*

# After The Banquet

## *A One-Act Comedy in Three Scenes*

DRAMATIS PERSONAE

Du Qingchuan, a drunkard
Xu Xiaobo, another drunkard
Busboys A and B
Mrs. Du
Mrs. Xu
A Maid in the Du household
A Relative of the maid

### ACT I | SCENE ONE
**In the Restaurant**

*Before the curtain rises, we hear a cacophony of voices calling "See you tomorrow!" and the patter of many footsteps. We also hear the rumble of cars starting up and driving off, and the clinking of dishes being cleared away. The curtain then rises to reveal a private room in a restaurant and part of an external staircase leading out of it. The time is 10:00 p.m., and a company banquet has just concluded. Enter Busboys.*

BUSBOY A:

Today's got me beat! I can barely walk!

BUSBOY B:

How exhausting. A ton of guests, and all of them drunk as lords.

BUSBOY A:

Today hasn't been so bad, though. At least we didn't have any trouble in sending all those drunks packing.

BUSBOY B:

What's this charcoal basket doing here?

*Busboy B goes to move a charcoal basket beneath a table when suddenly the basket moves, startling him.*

BUSBOY A:

What is it?

BUSBOY B:

There's something moving in that charcoal basket.

BUSBOY A:

(*Goes over and looks.*) Hey, it's Mr. Du. I thought he'd already gone home. Turns out he's been lying here.

BUSBOY B:

Mr. Du, everyone's gone home!

BUSBOY A:

Don't just lie there—hurry and get up!

Du Qingchuan:

(*Extends a hand.*) Stop! I can't drink any more.

Busboy B:

No one's pressing you to drink. Didn't you hear all those telephone calls just now? They must have been for this Mr. Du. I answered the phone five or six times.

Busboy A:

I answered the phone seven or eight times too. I hear his wife's a jealous one. She must have been the caller.

Busboy B:

In that case, since he's refusing to get up, let's trick him and tell him his wife's come to get him.

Busboy A:

Great, great! Mr. Du, your wife's here for you.

Du Qingchuan:

(*Jumps up.*) She is?! I really got too drunk today; that's why I'm out so late. (*Walks on unsteady legs.*)

Busboy B:

Look, he jumped up as soon as he heard his wife was here.

Du Qingchuan:

Where is she?

Busboy B:

She's not here; we tricked you.

Du Qingchuan:

You tricked me? You scared the heck out of me!

Busboy B:

If we hadn't, you never would have gotten up. Woah—here's another one! (*Finds another person lying by the railing.*)

Busboy A:

Isn't this Mr. Xu? Get up!

Xu Xiaobo:

(*Waves his hand.*) Get offa me! Let me lie down a tick.

Busboy B:

No way! Everyone's gone home. We need to clean up.

Du Qingchuan:

Hey, Xiaobo!

Xu Xiaobo:

Qingchuan, it's you!

Du Qingchuan:

I thought I was the only one left. With the both of us here I'm not lonely any more.

Xu Xiaobo:

Let's have a drink. Wine!

Busboy A:

No, no, no, no. No more wine today.

Xu Xiaobo:

(*Stands up, produces a wine jug, and shakes it.*) I've still got a bit left. Here you go … !

*Du Qingchuan goes over and the two start drinking. The two Busboys continue taking turns clearing dishes.*

Xu Xiaobo:

I moved into the house next door to yours yesterday, but my wife hasn't been over to your place yet to pay her respects to Mrs. Du.

Du Qingchuan:

We haven't come over to congratulate you on the move yet either.

Xu Xiaobo:

I caught a glimpse of your wife yesterday—what a beauty! You've been lucky in love.

Du Qingchuan:

She may have a pretty face, but she's got a nasty disease that I just can't stand.

Xu Xiaobo:

Ha ha! VD?

Du Qingchuan:

Don't be absurd!

Xu Xiaobo:

Some secret illness, then?

Du Qingchuan:

Wrong again. She suffers from intense jealousy.

Xu Xiaobo:

You're lucky she's so jealous!

Du Qingchuan:

What's so lucky about having a fearsomely jealous wife?

Xu Xiaobo:

You're lucky all right! That wife of mine is so devoid of jealousy it breaks my heart. I once duped her by telling her that I was on intimate terms with a prostitute and wanted to take her as a concubine. When she heard this she became delighted and said, "That'll mean another person at home to keep me from getting lonely." Where's the fun in that? That's why I say you're lucky to have a jealous wife.

Du Qingchuan:

It's no good if she's not jealous at all, but that kind of "vinegar" should be drunk in moderation. My wife goes way too far—she drinks it like tea! Just imagine: since I arrived at this restaurant she's telephoned for me seventy-three times!

Xu Xiaobo:

It'll be quite something having two women with opposite personalities living with only a wall between them.

*While the two are chatting, the Busboy rushes up and clears everything off the table.*

Xu and Du:

Hey, we hadn't finished yet! (*They give chase.*)

*Scene change.*

## SCENE TWO
### In Du Qingchuan's House

*On the stage is the living room, with the front door of the house on the left-hand side. The Maid is in a corner of the room making a phone call. She turns the dial and shouts into the receiver but gets no answer from the operator. Mrs. Du is sitting down.*

Mrs. Du:
Don't you even know how to make a phone call?

Maid:
They're not answering.

Mrs. Du:
If you keep dialing they're bound to answer.

Maid:
There's really no answer.

Mrs. Du:
You're hopeless. Yell louder!

*The Maid dials and yells so loud she nearly cries.*

Mrs. Du:
What kind of noise is that? Horrible! (*Stands up, huffily pushes the Maid aside, and dials the phone herself.*) Hello, operator? Why aren't you putting me through? It's already past midnight and one of my family members hasn't returned home yet. Put me through immediately to Number 2641, Heaven Above Restaurant. Why not? Inexcusable! (*Dials so viciously that she accidentally rips off the rotary dialer.*)

Maid:

Ma'am, the phone's broken.

*Mrs. Du puts the phone down and storms out of the room. Alarmed, the Maid walks over to the door, only to run into Mrs. Xu from next door standing there blankly. Seeing her there, the Maid lowers her head and curtseys.*

Mrs. Du:

What do you want? Are you here looking for my husband?

Mrs. Xu:

No. I just moved next door yesterday. My husband's name is Xu Xiaobo. I came to your house to offer our neighborly greetings.

Mrs. Du:

So it's the lady of the house from next door. Please excuse my lack of courtesy.

Mrs. Xu:

Likewise.

Mrs. Du:

Why are you standing here?

Mrs. Xu:

Because my husband hasn't come home yet.

Mrs. Du:

What? Your husband's not home yet either?

Mrs. Xu:

That's right.

Mrs. Du:

What could they be doing out at a time like this? Men never think about how lonely their wife is at home. They're such horrible beasts!

Mrs. Xu:

But men are obliged to attend social engagements like this one. They can't only concern themselves about things at home.

Mrs. Du:

What are you talking about, sister? How could you be so unconcerned? And what are you going to do about the situation? Don't you have a problem with your husband leaving his wife at home by her lonesome while he goes out carousing with sing-song girls?

Mrs. Xu:

He can't help it if that's what his social obligations call for.

Mrs. Du:

Ridiculous! (*She stomps her foot; Mrs. Xu recoils in alarm.*) With an attitude like that, do you think you deserve to be called lady of the house? I've learned that if you don't keep your man on a tight leash he'll slip out on you. How could you let him go messing around and just excuse it as being his "social obligations"? Don't you keep an eye on him at all? As soon as my husband comes home, I won't be finished with him till I've bitten through his windpipe! When mine's done I'll come over to your house to help you deal with yours. Don't hold back: scratch him on his face or do wherever you need to.

*Mrs. Du's willingness to help other people make a scene scares Mrs. Xu into fleeing back to her own house.*

Mrs. Du:

Worthless piece of garbage. (*Exits.*)

*While doing a little straightening up, the Maid has come closer to eavesdrop on their conversation.*

Maid:

She's really something!

*Enter Maid's Relative, carrying a sack.*

Relative:

Anyone home?

Maid:

(*Runs to the front door.*) My goodness—it's you! Why are you here at such a late hour?

Relative:

Haven't gone to bed yet? It's so late. I had originally planned on coming tomorrow morning.

Maid:

You came at just the right time. I was just thinking of quitting.

Relative:

What? Didn't you just start work today?

Maid:

I only arrived at suppertime, but by evening I'd had enough.

Relative:

How could you be so impatient?

Maid:

You have no idea what a jealous witch my mistress is. She's more than I can handle! If I have to work here one more day I might kill myself!

Relative:

What does her being jealous have to do with you?

Maid:

Today the master went out to some banquet, and in two hours she made seventy-five phone calls!

Relative:

Seventy-five calls—that's quite a precise memory you have.

Maid:

Later, would you believe it, she actually broke the phone. And as if that's not enough, she's planning to go help the lady next door fight her husband when he comes home. I haven't yet seen what kind of person the master is, but I don't see any way I can continue working here.

Relative:

It's already late. See how things look in the morning.

Maid:

I won't wait till tomorrow. I'm getting out of here tonight.

Relative:

But it's 1 A.M.!

Maid:

I don't care if it's two! If I can't find a place to sleep, I'll walk the streets all night if I have to. I'm sorry, but you should take your bag and leave. You don't want to fall into the mistress's clutches when she returns.

*The Relative has no choice but to pick up his bag and leave. The Maid is about to exit too when Xu Xiaobo, who lives next door, enters drunk, having muddle-headedly stumbled in the wrong door.*

Xu Xiaobo:

I'm home.

*The Maid takes him to be the master of the house.*

Maid:

You got home safely.

Xu Xiaobo:

Who are you?

Maid:

I just started work today.

Xu Xiaobo:

So you're the new maid. Where's the missus?

Maid:

The mistress was so worried that the master was out late that she went out to the street.

Xu Xiaobo:

What? She was worried that I wasn't back early and went out to fetch me? Now that's something! Well, I'm going to hit the sack. Is the bed made?

Maid:

It's been ready and waiting for you for a while now.

Xu Xiaobo:

Then I'm going to bed.

Maid:

Yes, get some rest.

Xu Xiaobo:

Give me a hand.

*The Maid supports Xu Xiaobo as he walks into the bedroom and then runs back out. Mrs. Du returns.*

Maid:

The master's back.

Mrs. Du:

What? He's back? Where is he?

Maid:

He's gone to sleep.

Mrs. Du:

Why did you let him go to sleep?

Maid:

He said he wanted to sleep, so I helped him into the bedroom to sleep.

Mrs. Du:

You helped my husband into the bedroom?

MAID:

Yes.

MRS. DU:

The moment I leave the house, you go and pull a trick like that? (*She raises her eyebrows and explodes in anger, scaring the wits out of the Maid.*) You wretch! How dare you!? (*Comes over to beat the Maid.*)

MAID:

I didn't do anything, ma'am!

*The Maid ducks blows from Mrs. Du, who chases her around. In the midst of the uproar, Du Qingchuan returns home.*

DU QINGCHUAN:

What's going on? What's this racket?

*The two separate, and the Maid runs away. Seeing that it's her husband, Mrs. Du hits the roof.*

MRS. DU:

A fine one you are! Making me stay home by my lonesome, and never coming home. I've never been so miserable! (*Grabs him.*)

DU QINGCHUAN:

Let go, let go! What are you doing?

MRS. DU:

You think I'm going to let you go? If I do, you'll leave again.

*Mrs. Du tries to bite his neck. As the two of them fight, Xu Xiaobo calls out from the bedroom.*

Xu Xiaobo:

Tea!

*Both startle. Mrs. Du suddenly forgets her jealousy and hides next to her husband in shock. Puzzled, Du Qingchuan stares at his wife.*

Xu Xiaobo:

Tea!

Du Qingchuan:

Oh, very nice! You stay here and don't move.

*Du Qingchuan steps into the bedroom and has a look, then comes back out and grabs his wife.*

Du Qingchuan:

This is rich.

Mrs. Du:

What?

Du Qingchuan:

Whose is this? (*He throws a tortoise shell comb onto the table.*)

Mrs. Du:

It's mine.

Du Qingchuan:

What is this comb doing on the floor by the bed?

Mrs. Du:

It was in the bedroom?

Du Qingchuan:

Still putting up a front?

Mrs. Du:

I know. It must have fallen to the floor when I was making the bed just now.

Du Qingchuan:

Bullshit!

*Mrs. Du is shocked.*

Du Qingchuan:

This comb isn't the only thing in the bedroom. There's also a man under the covers. You've got nothing left to say.

Mrs. Du:

Ah!

Du Qingchuan:

Shut your mouth, you hussy! Get out of my sight!

Mrs. Du:

What are you on about? I haven't done anything wrong!

Du Qingchuan:

Things are this far gone and you're still trying to make excuses? There's a man in the bed—what more proof do you want?

Mrs. Du:

I didn't know that. I was out just now. Only the maid was home.

Du Qingchuan:

How dare you open your mouth? Wait till I drag him out here and we'll see whether or not you confess your guilt.

Mrs. Du:

Go ahead! Get the story straight, then we'll talk.

Xu Xiaobo:

I need a drink. Bring me some tea!

Du Qingchuan:

It's tea you want, is it?

*Du Qingchuan rushes into the room and drags Xu Xiaobo out.*

Xu Xiaobo:

How dare you treat me like this!

Du Qingchuan:

Brazen scoundrel! (*Looks at his face.*)

Yikes! Brother Xiaobo!

Xu Xiaobo:

Yikes! Brother Qingchuan! What are you doing in my house?

Du Qingchuan:

In *your* house? This is *my* house!

Xu Xiaobo:

Aiyo! (*Looks around.*) Really: I just moved here and I was drunk, so I got things mixed up.

Du Qingchuan:

What ... ?

Mrs. Du:

You know him?

Du Qingchuan:

This is our next door neighbor, Mr. Xu.

Mrs. Du:

Huh?!

Du Qingchuan:

Bring out the wine and let's have a drink, then. Scratch everything I said just now.

*Mrs. Du, no longer jealous, obeys her husband's command and goes to prepare the wine.*

Du Qingchuan:

Brother Xiaobo, let's get smashed.

Xu Xiaobo:

I could use it. I was just starting to sober up.

Du Qingchuan:

Bring out the wine! Jump to it!

*Mrs. Du reenters with wine and food.*

*Scene change.*

## SCENE THREE
### Xu Xiaobo's House

*The room furnishings are much like those of the Du residence. Mrs. Xu is doing needlework under the lamp, waiting for her husband to come home. After a short while, she dozes off. Suddenly laughter erupts from the other side of the wall, startling her awake. She puts her ear up to the wall and listens.*

Mrs. Xu:
That's my husband's voice!

*A rooster crows and the electric light goes out. A distant factory whistle sounds.*

*Curtain.*

# The Horse's Tail

## *A Farce*

DRAMATIS PERSONAE

Man
His Wife
His Neighbor
Driver of Horse Carriage
Horse

*Upstage is a tiny room; downstage is an empty space in front of the front door.*

*Man, the occupant of the room, is alone onstage. He yawns.*

Man:
The last few days have really been a drag. There's nothing to do to pass the time. Hey!

Wife:
(*From within the room.*) Coming! (*Enter Wife.*) What is it?

Man:
Bring my fiddle[1] out here.

---

1. The Chinese *huqin* is a two-stringed instrument, which is stood vertically and bowed horizontally.

Wife:

You're going to play your fiddle again?

Man:

There's absolutely nothing to do. Might as well play a few tunes.

Wife:

Don't. It's so noisy.

Man:

What's the harm in making a little noise?

*Wife goes to get the fiddle.*

Wife:

Play, then.

Man:

What are you doing inside?

Wife:

I'm frying broad beans.

Man:

What's this? The mice nibbled a few strands off the bow of my fiddle. How am I supposed to play with the little that's left?

*Enter Driver, leading a horse.*

Driver:

Excuse me, do you mind if I tie up my horse here? I'll be back in a moment.

*Exit Driver. Wife goes back inside.*

MAN:

Hey! How could you tie your horse up here? You're blocking my doorway, and pretty soon the ground'll be covered in horse shit and horse piss. This isn't the place to tie up a horse! Where did that driver go? While he's gone, I'll take a few strands of horse hair to string my bow. Just the thing I need!

*Man looks in all directions; seeing that no one is around, he walks behind the horse and plucks five or six hairs from the horse's tail.*

*Enter Neighbor.*

NEIGHBOR:

Hey!

MAN:

Aiyo! You scared the heck out of me. So it's you.

NEIGHBOR:

It's me.

MAN:

What's the idea, tiptoeing around scaring people like that?

NEIGHBOR:

What are you up to?

MAN:

I was pulling a few hairs from this horse's tail.

NEIGHBOR:

What?! Pulling hairs from a horse's tail? … Yikes! That means trouble.

Man:

What sort of trouble?

Neighbor:

Goodness! You don't know? Pulling hairs from a horse's tail—how horrible! You mean you really don't know?

Man:

What on earth is wrong?

Neighbor:

Hey! If I weren't here to tell you, you'd have no idea what happens when you pull hairs from a horse's tail.

Man:

I don't understand.

Neighbor:

No wonder. You'd have to be clueless to do something like that. You wouldn't have *dared* if you'd known what would happen. This is too much for me; I'm going home. Bye.

Man:

Hold on.

Neighbor:

What is it?

Man:

Don't be in such a rush to leave. You said I'd only do something like this if I didn't understand something. What should I be worried about? What's the big deal about pulling a few strands from a horse's tail?

Neighbor:

Forget it, forget it. Just drop it.

Man:

You can't *not* tell me. You absolutely *have* to tell me what's wrong with pulling hairs from a horse's tail.

Neighbor::

What's it to you? You did this because you didn't know any better. If you had known you might not have done it.

Man:

That's why I'm asking you what the big deal is. Tell me.

Neighbor:

So you want me to tell you? I didn't come by this knowledge for free. I only learned after paying my dues. But my situation was different from yours. You're an old friend, so I'd never take your money. Forget taking your money—I wouldn't accept anything you offered me. How about this: treat me to a jug of wine and I'll tell you.

Man:

Wine?

Neighbor:

That's right.

Man:

Fine. How much do you want?

Neighbor:

It's up to you.

MAN:

One liter should be enough, then.

NEIGHBOR:

So stingy! Only one liter? That's not enough!

MAN:

Two liters, then. You should be able to tell me for a couple of liters.

NEIGHBOR:

It's all you can afford anyway. Two liters it is.

MAN:

Come have a seat inside.

*The two go inside.*

MAN:

Hey!

*Enter Wife.*

WIFE:

What is it?

MAN:

Go buy us two liters of wine. (*Exit Wife.*) … Now you can instruct me.

NEIGHBOR:

Not so fast. Let's wait till your wife returns. It wouldn't be worth anything if I told you now. It's much more fun to talk while drinking. (*Reenter Wife.*) … Ah, your wife is back. Sorry for the trouble.

WIFE:

Don't mention it. Sorry there's nothing to eat.

NEIGHBOR:

Those fried broad beans would do the trick. Why don't you bring some of those over? Just one dish would be plenty. More than that would be too much. For a drinker, having too many beans at once dulls the flavor. But too few is no good either. It's best to have just enough at one go and then add more when they're gone.

*Wife brings over broad beans.*

NEIGHBOR:

Thank you, thank you. Is the wine warmed up?

MAN:

Yes.

NEIGHBOR:

Sorry for the bother.

MAN:

So, what happens when you pull hairs from a horse's tail?

NEIGHBOR:

No rush. Don't get impatient. I'll tell you over a leisurely cup of wine.

*Drinks one cup.*

Neighbor:

Now *that's* a fine wine. The snacks are good too. Some people like to have a bunch of pals around when they drink, but I'm happier drinking alone. When the first swig of wine reaches my throat it's like I've died and gone to Heaven. Just now I was just at Big Huang's at the foot of the bridge, and it was mealtime so he asked me if I'd eaten yet. I was feeling hungry so naturally I told him that I hadn't eaten, but he's not a drinker and I can't force someone who doesn't drink to treat me to a drink. But if I just ate his food and went home without having had a drink I wouldn't feel right either. If I'd had money in my pocket I could have sent someone in his family out to buy some wine, but it so happened that I hadn't brought any money with me. That was no good, so I had to go home. Never thought that I'd spot you pulling hairs from a horse's tail. *Wine coming up!* I said to myself. Ha ha! *When luck's a lady, don't say "maybe"!* I knew I could pull some wine from that horse's tail. Ahh … a *truly* fine wine!

Man:

Hey! Don't just sit there drinking and going on about how good the wine is. What's the deal? What's wrong with pulling hairs from a horse's tail?

Neighbor:

Not so fast. Don't be so pushy. How could someone as impatient as you ever hope to understand? Relax, take a deep breath, and listen while I tell you in good time. Pulling hair from a horse's tail is no small matter, and that's why I'm taking my time telling you while I enjoy my wine. Doesn't that sound good to you? Nothing in the entire world is more frightening than "not knowing." You didn't know, so you pulled out hairs from a horse's tail; if you had known, you wouldn't have done it. I used to be in the dark, too, and once I pulled out a strand of tail hair too. That's when someone told me that I was asking for trouble. I asked him again and again what the problem was, but he refused to tell me for free. That's why I ended up paying money to get him to tell me.

MAN:

Is that right?

NEIGHBOR:

There's a big difference between those in the know and stupid ignoramuses. Ha ha ha ha!

MAN:

You said it.

NEIGHBOR:

I sure did. I never thought … what, no more wine?

MAN:

You've been downing cup after cup. Of course it's gone.

NEIGHBOR:

Was that two liters? You must have been trying to fob me off with just a liter and a half.

MAN:

Don't be ridiculous.

NEIGHBOR:

Well, it's really too little.

MAN:

If it's too little then it's too little.

Neighbor:

That's no good. The worst feeling in the world is to be half drunk and half sober. Bring another liter or I'll tell you next time. How can I tell you if I'm not drunk? I'm off.

Man:

Wait a minute, wait a minute. There's no way around it. Go buy some more.

*Wife goes off to buy wine.*

Neighbor:

Well then let's take our time and talk this over, shall we? My sincere apologies for having troubled you so much, but it can't be helped with a matter as serious as this. After all, I'm telling you out of the goodness of my heart.

Man:

If it's out of the goodness of your heart, then spit it out! I'm an impatient man. I can't bear it any longer. Tell me now before the wine comes. What will happen if you pull hairs from a horse's tail?

Neighbor:

You're right, you are impatient—not a whit of restraint! But that's how the world goes. Back in the day, if you had to go on a long journey you'd ride a horse, but now you can take a train, and if a train isn't fast enough you can take an airplane. Each is speedier and more impatient than the last …

Man:

Hey! I don't want to hear it! What a pain! What on earth will happen if you pull hairs out of a horse's tail?

*Wife returns with the wine.*

NEIGHBOR:

Don't rush me. Thanks for your trouble, sister. Which shop did this wine come from? It's superb! When it reaches my belly it makes me happier than I've ever felt. You're not a connoisseur so you wouldn't appreciate it. As the ancients put it, *When I'm drunk, the weighty matters of the world disappear.*[2] I like that line.

MAN:

What the hell are you babbling about? All I want is for you to tell me, but you keep putting me off. Now you're off on some tangent. What about the horse's tail?

NEIGHBOR:

Not so fast. Let me put back a cup first. That wine a moment ago was a bit cold, but this wine's nice and warm.

MAN:

Skip it! Pulling hairs from a horse's tail …

NEIGHBOR:

How do you expect to live long if your eyebrows are always on fire like this? Above all, a man's gotta remain calm. Watch me drain another cup. (*He drinks.*) Wonderful! Now I'll tell you all there is to know about what happens when you pull hairs from a horse's tail. When you hear it, you're sure to see the light.

MAN:

Then, if you pull a horse's tail …

---

2. A line from the Southern Song dynasty poet Lu You's 陸游 (1125–1210) poem "Autumn Meditations" 秋思.

Neighbor:

You're still so impatient. Uh oh—no more beans! Can't we get a little more wine too? Hey, sister! Here's the empty dish back.

Man:

Let her deal with that later. About that horse's tail …

Neighbor:

She might as well take the wine jug in too. Now that's what I call a good drink! (*Stands up and starts walking offstage.*)

Man:

Hey! Where are you going?

Neighbor:

I'm amblin' on home.

Man:

You're what?! What about all that about the horse's tail?

Neighbor:

That's right. I know, I know.

Man:

What do you mean "I know, I know?"

Neighbor:

I forgot.

Man:

How could you forget?! What happens if you pull hairs from a horse's tail?

NEIGHBOR:

If you pull hairs from a horse's tail …

MAN:

If you pull hairs from a horse's tail …

NEIGHBOR:

That is, if you pull out hairs from a horse's tail …

MAN:

*Yes?!?!*

NEIGHBOR:

You'll hurt the horse.

*Curtain.*

# Joke Names

*As you'll have noticed, Xu Zhuodai was fond of joke names. Here are examples of how I rendered a few of them into English, listed in the order in which they appear in this volume.*

| | | |
|---|---|---|
| Litman Deng | Deng Wengong 鄧文工 | Wengong suggests "literature worker"; I've opted for the more general "man of literature" |
| Tainted Fei | Fei Chunren 費純人 | *fei chunren* 非純人: impure person, or person with ulterior motives |
| Handsome Xiao | Xiao Bolian 蕭伯蓮 | Puns on both *xiao bailian* 小白臉, a derogatory term for a handsome, effeminate young man, and the Chinese name of George Bernard Shaw, Xiao Bona 蕭伯納 |
| Floozie Yang | Yang Lanwu 楊蘭塢 | *yang lanwu* 洋爛污: "Western moral depravity" |
| Chicken Ma | Ma Ruji 馬如雞 | Mimics the name of the historical *tanci* performer Ma Rufei 馬如飛 (Soaring Ma, 1851–1908) |
| I.M. Broke | Qian Kongru 錢空如 | No money; penniless |

| | | |
|---|---|---|
| Joe Kerr | Long Boxia 龍伯夏 | Pronounced in Shanghainese, sounds like 儂弗笑: don't laugh |
| Ngo Paw-wah | Mei Youquan 梅幽泉 | *meiyou quan* 沒有權: no power/authority |
| Monsieur Misérable | Qiong Deheng 瓊德亨 | *qiong de hen* 窮得很: extremely poor |
| Herr Stonen-Broken | Fei Nixu 斐尼虛 | sounds like "finished" |
| Mr. Skint | Bidi xunsi 畢滴遜斯 | a version of the Shanghainese pidgin phrase *bie di shengsi* 癟的生斯 that sounds like both (1) "empty cents," meaning penniless, and (2) the "life of a bum" 癟三[1] |
| Hongari-san | Dakou kongfu 大口空腹 | "Big mouth, empty belly" |
| Pye N.D. Skye | Yeye Wu 耶耶烏 | *ye* is an interrogative particle; *wu* sounds like *wu* 無 (nothing) and appears in *wutuobang* 烏托邦 (utopia), so this delegate's proposal suggests a questionable fantasy |
| Eminent Li | Li Gongding 李公鼎 | Li, who is esteemed by the public; as mentioned in the note, *Gongding* alludes to Lord Mao's Pot (Maogong-ding, a famous relic), which, combined with Li, suggests the name Li Ah Mao. |

1. See Wang Zhongxian 汪仲賢 (text), Xu Xiaoxia 許曉霞 (illustrations), *Shanghai suyu tushuo* 上海俗語圖說 (Shanghai Slang, Illustrated and Explained) (Shanghai: Shenzhou tushu gongsi, 1935), entry #42 (癟三), pp. 81–83.

| | | |
|---|---|---|
| Roll N. Doh | Jin Mantang 金滿堂 | "House filled with gold" |
| Kit D. Bouquet | Tan Laosan 談老三 | The name suggests "to be #3," as in the phrase: "When #1 and #2 fight, it's #3 who dies" (*laoda, lao'er dajia, laosan sile* 老大, 老二打架, 老三死了), or less literally: "When the big boys fight, it's other people who get hurt." Many Shanghainese slang terms for indigence or misfortune involve the number three. For example *biesan* 癟三 (bum), means an emaciated person who is "triple bare" 三光, having eaten up 吃光, used up 用光, and pawned away 當光 everything.[2] |
| Kway See Chen | Chen Jinping 陳錦屏 | sounds like *shenjingbing* 神經病, neurotic |
| Dandy Chen | Chen Weimei 陳維美 | Weimei 維美 sounds like *weimei* 唯美, aesthete |
| Lechy Lao | Lao Boshi 勞伯施 | sounds like *lao bu si* 老不死, a person who has outlived his or her usefulness; can also refer specifically to an old man who chases or lusts after young women |
| Shameless | Bu Xiaolian 卜效廉 | pun on *bu yao lian* 不要臉: shameless |
| Parrot | Ma Yingwu 馬英嫵 | [*ma* 罵] *yingwu* 鸚鵡: [cursed for being a] parrot |

2. See ibid., entry #88 (三光), pp. 178–181.

# Publication Notes

Xu Zhuodai was a prolific writer whose literary career lasted from the 1900s to the 1950s. His most prolific period was during China's Republican era (1911–1949), when he published stories, essays, playscripts, editorials, jokes, poems, translations, advice columns, and photographs in scores of magazines and newspapers. Many original collections of his works still survive. Some of his stories and jokes have been reprinted in several contemporary collections; his plays, to my knowledge, have never been anthologized. Between the founding of the People's Republic in 1949 and his death in 1958, Xu wrote memoirs and works of nonfiction, mostly about Shanghainese farce (*huaji xi*) and about the drama scene in "old" Shanghai. His fiction was mostly neglected during the Mao era but became a subject of academic research with the release of Wei Shaochang's 魏紹昌 (1922–2000) anthology *Research Materials on the Mandarin Ducks and Butterflies School* 鴛鴦蝴蝶派研究資料 (Shanghai: Shanghai wenyi chubanshe) in 1962. My translations are based on the original editions published in the Shanghai magazines listed below. All of the stories collected here, with the exception of "Plagiarist in Western Dress," have been anthologized in a collection edited by Fan Boqun 范伯群 (1931–2017), which I have also consulted: *Representative Works of the Master of Comedy, Xu Zhuodai* 滑稽大師徐卓呆代表作 (Nanjing: Jiangsu wenyi chubanshe, 1996).

## AUTHOR'S PREFACE (*Zi Xu*自序)

*Xiaohua sanqian* 笑話三千 (Three Thousand Jokes). Shanghai: Zhongyang shudian, 1935, vol. 1, p. 1.

## STORIES

1. **Woman's Playthings** (*Nüxing de wanwu* 女性的玩物)
   *Hong meigui* 紅玫瑰 (Red Rose), vol. 5, issue 3 (2 Mar. 1928).
2. **The Fiction Material Wholesaler** (*Xiaoshuo cailiao pifasuo* 小說材料批發所)
   *Banyue* 半月 (The Half Moon Journal), vol. 1, issue 3 (15 Oct. 1921).
3. **The International Currency Reform Conference** (*Wanguo huobi gaizao dahui* 萬國貨幣改造大會)
   *Hong zazhi* 紅雜誌 (The Scarlet Magazine), issue 19 (1922).
4. **Plagiarist in Western Dress** (*Yangzhuang de chaoxijia* 洋裝的抄襲家)
   *Hong zazhi*, issue 33 (1923).
5. **Expose Plagiarism!** (*Gaofa chaoxi* 告發抄襲)
   *Hong zazhi*, issue 34 (1923).
6. **The Unofficial Story of Li Ah Mao** (*Li Amao waizhuan* 李阿毛外傳)
   The twelve stories in this series were published consecutively in the first twelve issues of the monthly magazine *Wanxiang* 萬象 (Wan hsiang), between July 1941 and June 1942:
   A. April Fool's Day 愚人節
   B. Turned Around 向後轉
   C. The Marketing Director 推廣部主人
   D. Han Emperor Gaozu's Washbasin 漢高祖的水盂
   E. Date Pits with Holes 有孔棗子核
   F. The Pearl Necklace 珠項圈

G. The Overnight Fortuneteller 隔夜算命
H. Please Exit Through the Back Door 請走後門出去
I. Moving Permit 搬出証
J. The Lockout 封鎖
K. Japanese School 日語學校
L. Seeking Lifelong Partner 徵求終身伴侶

## FARCES

1. **The Devil Messenger** (*Juhun shizhe* 拘魂使者)
   *Xiaoshuo shijie* 小說世界 (The Story World), vol. 1, issue 1 (5 Jan. 1923).
2. **A Father's Duty** (*Fuqin de yiwu* 父親的義務)
   *Xiaoshuo shijie*, vol. 2, issue 4 (1923).
3. **Marrying Indirectly** (*Jianjie jiehun* 間接結婚)
   *Xiaoshuo shijie*, vol. 1, issue 8 (1923).
4. **Upstairs, Downstairs: Two Couples** (*Shangxia liangdui* 上下兩對)
   *Xiaoshuo shijie*, vol. 1, issue 6 (9 Feb. 1923).
5. **After the Banquet** (*Yanhui hou* 宴會後)
   *Xiaoshuo shijie*, vol. 2, issue 1 (1924).
6. **The Horse's Tail** (*Ma wei* 馬尾)
   *Xiaoshuo shijie*, vol. 1, issue 13 (1924).

# Further Readings

## Writings by Xu Zhuodai in English Translation

"Cooper" (*Gu* 箍). Tr. William A. Lyell. *Two Lines: A Journal of Translation* (Spring 1994).

"Fantastically Fabulous" (*Shen wei jiamiao* 甚為佳妙). Tr. Maria Hongying Zheng and Sunny Yuchen Liu. *Renditions* 87/88 (Spring/Autumn 2017): 203–234.

"Men's Depravity Exposed" (*Chiluoluo de nanzi choutai* 赤裸裸的男子醜態). Tr. Timothy C. Wong. In Timothy C. Wong, ed. *Stories for Saturday: Twentieth Century Chinese Popular Fiction.* Honolulu: University of Hawaii Press, 2003, pp. 215–217.

"Opening Day Advertisement" (*Kaimu guanggao* 開幕廣告). Tr. Christopher Rea. *Renditions* 87/88 (Spring/Autumn 2017): 189–202.

"The Secret Room" (*Mimi shi* 秘密室). Tr. Christopher Rea. *Renditions* 77/78 (Spring/Autumn 2012): 78–86.

## Studies of Xu Zhuodai (aka Xu Banmei) in English

Altenberger, Roland. "The Female Knight as a Modern Girl: Xu Zhuodai's Comic *Xia* Novel *Nüxia hong kuzi.*" In *The Sword or the Needle: The Female Knight-errant (xia) in Traditional Chinese Narrative.* Bern: Peter Lang, 2009, 342–351.

Dong Xinyu. "The Laborer at Play: *Laborer's Love*, the Operational

Aesthetic, and the Comedy of Inventions." *Modern Chinese Literature and Culture* 20:2 (Fall 2008): 1–39.

Gimpel, Denise. "Discussing Modern Questions." In *Lost Voices of Modernity: A Chinese Popular Fiction Magazine in Context.* Honolulu: University of Hawaii Press, 2001.

Rea, Christopher. "Comedy and Cultural Entrepreneurship in Xu Zhuodai's '*Huaji* Shanghai.'" *Modern Chinese Literature and Culture* 20:2 (Fall 2008): 40–91.

_____. "Enter the Cultural Entrepreneur." In *The Business of Culture: Cultural Entrepreneurs in China and Southeast Asia, 1900–65*. Vancouver, BC: UBC Press, 2015, pp. 9–31.

_____. *The Age of Irreverence: A New History of Laughter in China.* Oakland, CA: University of California Press, 2015.

Yeh, Emily Yueh-Yu. "A Small History of *Wenyi*." In *The Oxford Handbook of Chinese Cinemas*. Ed. Carlos Rojas and Eileen Chow. Oxford University Press, pp. 225–249.

Zhang Yingjin. "Witness Outside History: Play for Alteration in Modern Chinese Culture." *Modernism/modernity* 20:2 (April 2013): 349–369.

Zhang Zhen. *An Amorous History of the Silver Screen: Shanghai Cinema, 1896–1937*. Chicago: University of Chicago Press, 2005.

# ABOUT THE AUTHOR

Xu Zhuodai (1880–1958) was an educator, playwright, author, comedian and cultural entrepreneur hailed in Republican-era Shanghai as "Charlie Chaplin of the East."

# ABOUT THE TRANSLATOR

Christopher Rea is Professor of Asian Studies at the University of British Columbia and the author of several studies of modern Chinese literary and cultural history, including *The Age of Irreverence: A New History of Laughter in China* (University of California Press, 2015). He is cotranslator, with Bruce Rusk, of *The Book of Swindles: Selections from a Late Ming Collection* (Columbia University Press, 2017).

eap.einaudi.cornell.edu/publications

CPSIA information can be obtained
at www.ICGtesting.com
Printed in the USA
LVHW081938141119
637261LV00015B/26/P

9 781939 161048